THE JOURNEY
OF THE FORGOTTEN
KAHUL

THE JOURNEY OF THE FORGOTTEN KAHUL

By

S.E. BAILEY

First published by LAUREN MOOI Publishing 2020

Copyright © 2020 by S.E. Bailey

S.E. Bailey asserts the moral right to be identified as the author of this work in accordance with the Copyright Act 98 of 1978.
First Edition November 2020 in paperback
ISBN: 978-0-620-90971-6

www.laurenmooipublishing.com

LAUREN MOOI

PUBLISHING

CHAPTER 1

TALES OF TIME

It was a rainy Saturday afternoon; I was sitting at the window while my two young children. Bram who is 13 years old and Seth who is 10 years old. They were playing on the carpet with their toys. I turned to look at my children as the rain trickled on the windowpane. We lived in an ordinary three-bedroom countryside house in a small mining town. People were friendly and most knew each other because of the mine, the Grit Mine as it was known. I was never a city girl; I grew up as an only child in a town just a few hours away that not many people know of and that was okay with me. As long as my family and I were happy, we were not too bothered with other folks. As the boys played, I remembered the day my husband Zack carved the wooden horse my son was playing with. I also remembered the horse had a distinguished smell when it got wet. Zack made it clear to the boys that they should not get the toy wet. Just the thought of that smell affected me instantly. My very hypersensitivity is due to my pregnancy. I am at the very last stage of my pregnancy and some smells still affect me. For a moment I drifted off into a daydream as drops of rain fell onto the windowsill, that's when I felt my unborn child move. What a delightful feeling it was; as though my baby had just woken up, stretching his or her legs. I smiled at the notion. My husband and I are not very wealthy. We couldn't afford the opportunity to note what sex the baby is, but we're happy that the unborn child would be healthy like our boys were when they were born and that's all that matters. It's a month before I give birth and I am very excited, as are the children. My husband Zack worked late most of the time, and we grew accustomed to it. He always tried to get extra shifts, working in the mines, to be able to provide a better life for our family.

I got up slowly from the window and made my way to the kitchen, to pre-heat the supper I prepared earlier in the day. On my way to the kitchen, I heard the front door open, and Zack walked in. Zack was an average height man with a strong build. And his dark brown hair was always cut short. He had a smile that would captivate anyone's heart on a rainy day, and those deep green eyes will trap anyone who dares to look at them. I am shocked to see him home so early, but didn't ask any questions.

"Supper will be ready soon my love," I said with a smile. Which was not reciprocated. Zack had a strange look on his face and only nodded his head to acknowledge me. The rain had stopped.

"Ma?" My eldest son Bram asked, "Please can we go outside to play?" I looked at Zack, thinking he might say something, but nothing was said. I turned to face Bram and responded,

"Okay boys, put on your long boots and rain coats and be inside just before sunset." Seth my youngest son, called out to Bram, "You always slow, come on hurry up, in case Ma changes her mind." I smiled and went on setting the table. Before they headed outside, I turned and said to Bram,

"Young man, look after your brother and don't go too far, it will be dark soon." As Bram walked towards the front door, he turned and looked over his brother's shoulder and smiled. Bram loved his younger brother and will always look after him and protect him. His father told him;

"When I am gone, you are the man of this house young man, never forget that." As the children left the house, I started unpacking the plates from the shelve to set the table and my unborn baby started moving again. Zack headed towards our bedroom when I called out to him and said,

"Our little one is very busy tonight, maybe our baby knows we are having chicken and beans, my favourite." I received no reply from him as he walked towards the bedroom. I called out again,

"Are you ok my love? Is there anything bothering you that I should know of?" He made his way without any reply into the room and sat on the edge of the bed, with his back facing the door. I walked over to him. Our room is very dull with little furniture. It had a double bed, clothing cupboard and the little dressing cupboard that I got from my great-aunt and uncle.

"Zack!" I exclaimed in a firm voice.

"What is wrong? Why are you avoiding me and the children this evening?" Zack sat on the edge of the bed, and slowly turned towards me and said,

"I'm okay my dear, I just had a very strange day at work." I made my way towards him to comfort him, and as I kissed him on the forehead, he smiled and said,

"I am okay. And happy I'm at home with my family." While comforting him, I said.

"Once you have taken a shower you will feel much better and relaxed. When you are done you can come help me dish up." Then headed for the door.

"Oh, my love. You know exactly how to make me feel better." I turned around and gave him a wink and made my way back to the kitchen while he got ready for a shower. I could hear the children scuffling and laughing outside, I looked at the clock and called out to them to come back inside. The kitchen's back door opened and Bram walked in. I could see the frown on his face.

"Ma…" Bram sighed, "Please give us another 10 minutes, we having so much fun with the puppy we found…" Bram quickly tries to change his words, "…the puppy doll we found." But I already knew what he meant.

"Bram…" I had a not-kidding-look on my face, "What have I taught you about fibbing?"

"Sorry Ma. We were going to tell you, but you know Papa might not let us keep him."

"Bram Hanson! Go fetch your brother and wash up for supper immediately!"

"But Ma, what about the puppy? It's cold and wet outside and his all alone." I looked at Bram annoyed and said, "Just fetch your brother, and let me worry about the puppy." Bram turned towards the front door, walking with his head down. And as he opens the door, he turned back around, looking towards the kitchen with a sad face, thinking I might not accept the puppy they found. But his look of despair never dissuaded me. Bram disappeared through the doorway, into the dim light as the sun was setting. I thought to myself while standing in the kitchen looking out through the window; we barely making ends meet, we cannot afford a puppy. Although, keeping the puppy could be a blessing for the children, which may just teach them about responsibility. I walked towards the kitchen's back door as the door opened and the boys entered, one by one. As the boys took their boots off and I noticed Seth kept his coat on. Instantly I knew my boys were up to something.

"Seth?" I called out

"Yes Ma?" he replied.

"Why are you not taking your coat off?"

"Oh Ma," he continued,

"I will hang it in the bathroom, it just got a little wet, no need to worry." I looked at my son with my not-kidding-look and said,

"Seth Hanson, what have I taught you of fibbing? What is under that coat of yours?" Seth looked at me with a sad face, and as I questioned him, I heard a little sneezing sound coming from Seth.

"Seth are you okay my boy?"

"Yes Ma, I'm okay. It wasn't me"

"If it wasn't you, then who was it?" I asked. Seth had a guilty look on his face as he responded to my question.

"Well Ma, it came from my coat," and as he opened his coat, a beautiful little puppy was sitting in Seth's left arm hidden in the coat.

"Oh Seth" I said with a silent sigh.

"You boys should know better than to bring a stray puppy into the house before asking me. Stray animals are known to carry all sorts of diseases, and I cannot take the risk of catching anything from strays at this late stage in my pregnancy." Seth answered, "Ma, his just a baby and he doesn't have a home. We will love him and take care of him, we promise." Bram and Seth both stood in the kitchen with a very displeasing look on their faces. And they could probably tell I was considering it. Together they started shouting at the top of their lungs. "We promise! We promise Ma!" Seth with his little soft voice stepped forward and said,

"Ma, we promise we will take care of him and we are sorry for not telling you, but please can we keep him?" I lifted my hands and waved it in the air while saying,

"Hush child, hush! I have to ask your father first before we can keep him." At that moment, I heard rumbling coming from Bram's stomach.

"Are you hungry my big man?" Bram answered,

"Yes Ma, but please can I share my food with the puppy?" I looked at Bram and said; go wash up first so we can eat. Afterwards you may see to the puppy." Seth rushed towards the bathroom to wash his hands, but Bram stood and looked at me with sad eyes.

"Bram?" I said softly, "Why so sad my boy?"

"Ma..." he said as he continued, "I don't know when last the puppy ate. He must be starving and it's not right for me to eat, knowing he is hungry." I looked at my son, feeling very proud to see how much he has grown. And with so much empathy for an animal.

"Okay. On top of the cupboard in my bedroom there's a bottle of shampoo. Give me the puppy, so that you can go and fetch it." Bram quickly rushed towards the bedroom to get the shampoo and ran into his father as Zack made his way out of the bedroom.

"Sorry Papa, I thought you were still in the bathroom."

"No my boy, I'm on my way to help your mother. Is there anything I can help you with?"

"Yes Papa, mother said I should get the shampoo for our new dog. Seth and I found him, and Ma said we can keep him."

"Oh, did she now? Well let me go meet this new dog of yours." Zack helped Bram reach for the shampoo on top of the cupboard and they both made their way towards the kitchen. I called out to Bram and to my surprise Zack and Bram walked into the kitchen together, with Zack holding the shampoo bottle. He looked at me with a soft smile on his face and said,

"So, what is this I hear about a new dog?" Bram immediately looked at his father and thought he might disapprove about the dog but instead Zack said,

"So where is the new fellow?" In the corner close to the oven, laid a small little pointy ear black puppy with a brown and grey tail.

"Oh, there he is. I have to say he looks quiet." Zack mentioned. The excitement on Bram's face grew as he said.

"Papa can we keep him please?"

"Yes, but as long as you take care of him." I turned towards Zack and said,

"My dear I told the boys about the responsibility that comes with a dog and well I do believe they will keep their promise." We stood in the kitchen talking while Seth overheard us and came running in from the bathroom.

"Yes, me too. I will keep my promise Ma." I smiled at his enthusiasm.

"Bram, you go wash up and I will give the puppy something to eat to fill his stomach." I had baby milk formular in the cupboard, which I made for the puppy. I was preparing the milk while Zack and Seth sat down at the table. They both couldn't keep their eyes of the dog. I gave the puppy some warm thick milk. Bram appeared and said,

"I am done." Again, I could hear Bram's stomach grumble.

"My boy please sit, Zack please can you start dishing up for all of us while I will get something for the puppy to sleep in." I then went to the loft and found an old reef basket that Nana used to store her wool. I cleaned it out and placed some old linen in it, to make a warm bed for him to sleep in next to the oven. As soon as I put the basket down, the puppy got into it immediately, to have a nap. I was surprised at how quickly the puppy made himself comfortable, and incredibly pleased that he did.

"Come my dear sit and relax, don't worry too much about the new puppy. After supper the boys and I will clear up the kitchen and then we can give the puppy a nice warm bath while you put your feet up and relax for the evening. What do you boys say about that?" Zack turned to ask and both quickly responded "Yes, yes please Papa." When supper ended, Zack told the boys to go prepare the bath. I stayed seated at the table and could not help thinking what was bothering him when he first arrived home.

"My dear, why did you look so down when you came home this afternoon?" I asked. He slowly placed the plates in the sink and turned towards me with a sad look on his face and said,

"Well, my love, today at work my manager told me about a new clearing path they were going to make in the woods. When I went to see the site, I couldn't help the emotional hurt I felt.

It was as though I could feel the pain of the trees and plants that was being cut down." As he told me the story, I felt a sharp pain. This pain forced out a loud cry. While rubbing my tummy, I whispered gently, "Not now baby, it's not your time yet."

"Is it time? Are you okay?" I could see the concern on his face as I reassured him.

"No I'm okay, it's not yet time, just a cramp." Still with concern on his face, he said.

"Must've been that silly story. I'm sorry my dear, maybe it was just my imagination playing tricks on me."

"It's okay, no need to apologize. At least you could talk about it and get it off your chest. If you still feel like talking about it later, we can."

"No all is fine, it's just a silly story."

"Okay. Off you go, before the boys start worrying about this puppy bath."

"Come boy," he said, calling out to the puppy. He laid in his basket and looked at me, as though he were waiting for me to say something.

"My dear, just look; his so small and already lazy." I looked at the puppy and I said,

"Go on boy. Go with Zack for your bath." And the puppy jumped out of his basket and walked towards Zack.

"Okay that's weird, but maybe not. At least he listens to someone in the house." And we both laughed. I got up and headed for the kettle to make some tea. While the kettle was boiling, I glanced through the backdoor window. I noticed that the backyard was extremely dark, which was very unusual. I decided not to make a fuss of it and rather not say anything. The kettle stopped and I made my tea. As I was stirring my cup of tea, I could swear I saw something moving close to the back porch. Oh no, do not talk yourself into something, I thought. Just relax and finish your tea. I sat down at the table and the puppy came running into the kitchen.

"Hello boy, are you nice and clean?" But he ran straight past me, towards the kitchen backdoor and started barking and growling.

"No boy, you cannot go out. You have to warm up first. Then I will take you outside, once I have finished my tea." The puppy turned, walked towards me and laid by my feet. Zack called out,

"I am just cleaning up the bathroom." He told the boys to go to their bedroom, preparing them for bedtime. I could hear the boys running towards their bedroom.

"Boys not so loud." Zack yelled.

"Okay Papa." Bram answered. Sitting at the kitchen table, I looked down at my feet and could see the puppy watching me closely.

"So, puppy. I have rules. No peeing in the house or doggy do either. I have enough cleaning going on around here. When you want to go outside, scratch the back door, okay? You get three meals per day, lots of cuddles and love." I let out a little giggle when I said cuddles and once those words were spoken, the puppy gave a little bark. I was taken by surprise at his positive response. And just then, looking at him, I could have sworn his eye colour changed.

"Puppy didn't you have black eyes? Your one eye is light brown, and your other is blue?" I looked at him and kept thinking; surely, I would've seen if his eyes were different or maybe I am tired, it has been such a long day. Zack walked into the kitchen joining me at the table.

"My love, are you feeling a bit better now? I really need you to relax more and since I am off for two weeks and the boys school holiday started today, we can have more family time together." I looked at him while he was speaking and I could see the tiredness in his eyes.

"Yes, that sounds like a wonderful plan." In that moment the boys all dressed ready for bed made their way into the kitchen. As they entered the kitchen, Seth asked,

"Ma, what should we call him?" I replied,

"I want you and your brother to dream about a name for him and you might wake up with his name in the morning." They both nodded their heads in agreeance.

"Ma, where's the puppy going to sleep?" I turned and looked at him and said,

"Why don't you ask him where he wants to sleep." The children excitingly each called the puppy to come towards them, but the puppy remained in his basket.

"Sorry boys" I said, "It seems he wants to sleep in his basket tonight. Off to bed with the two of you." The children made their way to their bedroom with me, and I tucked them in. Kissing each one on the forehead goodnight and left the room with the door halfway open. I walked back to the kitchen where I found Zack yawning and stretching.

"Oh my. Aren't you looking tired? You should call it a night my dear and go to bed. I will be there shortly. This little one is still wide awake." While rubbing my tummy.

"Sorry my love, this tiredness just came over me. I will lock up first." Zack locked up and went to bed. The puppy sat still in his basket like a good boy. I found that to be very strange to say the least. But I decided not to over think it. I turned towards the dog and said,

"Okay puppy, so it's only me, you and the almost baby. Puppy, do you want to pee?" The puppy got up, ran to the door and started scratching. I walked towards the backyard light switch close to the door and turned it on. The light was not that bright but at least I could see the three steps that led down the porch to the back garden. I opened the door and the puppy kept walking close to me. As I made my way slowly down the steps counting one by one. I got to the last step, looked around the back yard and noticed how dark and creepy it was. The only light that was shining, came from the moon. As it reflected, I could see Zack's shed where he kept all his tools and next to the garage there was an old skinny tree leaning onto the garage roof, first time I noticed that. I need to tell Zack to do something about it before it collapses onto the roof. I looked down and could see the puppy sniffing and looking back at me each time.

"Come on boy, get done. This back yard is giving me the heebie jeebies." I could swear I saw a strange figure standing next to the tree in the backyard. I brushed it off and thought my imagination or my eyes are playing tricks on me, because I am rather tired. I looked around again, towards the area where I thought I saw something. The puppy ran in the direction I was looking at, and within an instant I saw it again. I can't quite put my finger on it or explain what I saw because I have never seen it before, but what I can say is that it didn't feel like it was something normal. Then something strange happened; as the puppy's front paws touched the ground, he appeared to be magically transforming. From a puppy into a grown dog with just three steps. A light appeared to shine through him as he was transforming. He ran towards the back where something or someone was lurking, and he gave a heavy bark and it seems the thick darkness was lifted from the back yard. What was that

I just saw? My eyes wide open unable to blink, in the fear of missing out. I must be tired because that is not possible, I thought. And as quick as the darkness was lifted, he ran back to me. Once a puppy but now a grown adult dog with a black and white glistering coat. His tail was thick and more of a golden colour with his pointy black ears. His eye colour still so strange but brighter than before.

"What just happened?" I said to him as he sat in front of me.

"This can't be possible." I spoke in disbelief. He gave a soft bark, turned and ran to the other side of the house and disappeared around the corner.

"Here boy, here boy. Where are you going?" I called out to him still feeling so confused about what just happened. Then I thought, if I lost this dog the children will be so upset and disappointed. I couldn't understand why the dog didn't return and decided to go back into the house and wait. While walking towards the backdoor, I got a chilling cold breeze rushing past me and decided to call it a night. My boys are going to be so upset and they will blame me, what do I do? Okay, first thing tomorrow morning I will look for the dog. I'm not sure how I am going to explain to Zack what I just witnessed. I entered the back door and heard a knock at my front door. Who will knock this late, after 9pm? And again, I heard the knock. My bedroom door opened.

"Zack!" I said, "Thought you would be fast asleep by now. There's someone at the door." I said hesitantly. "Please go and see who it is." He looked at me and asked,

"Are you ok my love?" I decided not to mention anything about what I witnessed just yet.

"I lost our children's dog. I am really beginning to worry." Again, a knock at the door, for the third time.

"Maybe it's one of our neighbors needing help or returning our dog?" he continued as he walked towards the door. "Daina, please relax, everything will be fine."

"Yes Zack." I replied. Zack reached the front door and asked, "Who's there? What do you want?" There was no response to Zack's question. He asked again, "What do you want?" A soft bark came from the other side of the door and immediately he turned towards me and said, "You see no need to worry. It's the dog. Someone brought him back." Zack opened the door, and there was a familiar face.

"Uncle Pat, what a surprise. What are you doing here and at this time of the night?" I greeted him with a hug. Pat is my great-uncle and he loved me to bits. He is a tall well-presented man. He has thick black hair, with one grey spot in front of his forehead. He also wore round funny shaped glasses. And he always carried a pocket watch, visible by the chain attached to his waist coat.

"Oh, sorry Daina." Pat says, "I forgot someone." Pat stepped away and a big beautiful black German Shepard mix breed dog was sitting beside him.

"I found him on your grass and I thought he might belong to you."

"Please come in Uncle Pat." He noticed the confused looked on my face about the dog, but he ignored it and just gave me a wink and snapped his finger. Zack called the dog inside and started rubbing him.

"Oh boy you gave Daina such a fright this evening. She thought you ran away." He gave a little friendly bark in response to Zacks affection.

"So, what do you call him?" Pat asked. Strangely with no thought in mind I said,

"His name is Langos."

"Oh, what a nice name." Pat said. Zack turned to me and spoke.

"Yes, that is a nice strong name." And gave the dog a rub on his head. Full of energy, he turned from Zack and ran straight towards me. Instantly I felt calmness cover me, and my unborn baby started to settle in my womb. I still wonder why Zack could not recall that we had a puppy, just a few hours ago and not a grown dog. Instead, I decided not to say anything.

"So, Pat." I asked, "How long are you visiting us? The children will be very excited to see you in the morning when they wake."

"The reason why I am here, is because Nana asked about you and we could not reach you on the phone. I decided to come over instead and remind you of the visit you owe Nana and I. Especially since it is your birthday coming up soon."

"Oh yes, we had promised we will visit." Zack said. I turned to look at both of them and responded,

"Yes, but you all know I'm not much of a birthday person. It's getting late Uncle Pat; I will prepare a bed for you."

"No, my child, I have booked into the local hotel. I will see you early in the morning, my taxi is waiting for me outside."

"Okay Uncle Pat." I gave him a hug goodbye. Pat shook Zack's hand and said,

"Okay get some rest. Early start tomorrow morning. Your Nana will be happy to see all of you. Especially you Daina." Pat greeted, got into his taxi and drove off. Zack and I made our way to the bedroom and Langos made himself comfortable in the kitchen close to the oven.

"Daina, are you excited to see Nana this weekend? And the old house? I can't wait to take the kids to the river." Zack said, while closing the bedroom door.

"Oh yes, but I still have so many questions I would like to ask Nana about my childhood. I have so little memories. The only memory I have is playing in the woods. I must've been around 10 years old when Nana told me to never go past the big tree. I wonder why I can't remember anything else. It is a question I would like to ask Nana." As I got into bed Zack turned to me and said,

"Don't worry my dear you will have enough time to spend with Nana to have all your questions answered. Try and get some sleep." Eventually I fell asleep and dreamt about the woods. There were different lights that shined through the trees.

CHAPTER 2

THE JOURNEY OF THE BEGINNING

In the early hours of the morning Zack was woken up by a strange yet distinguished smell. He sat up straight in bed and I could sense he was awake and woke up myself.

"Zack? What's that smell?" I asked. "It smells like burnt rotten food coupled with a bad wooden smell."

"Yes, I know that smell from a long time ago. That old wooden horse, that's the smell it has when it gets wet. Remember when I found it in the woods? When we were kids? It only smelt when it got wet." That was strange, I thought.

"Yes Zack, I remember." I sat up. "Nana forbid us from going to that side of the woods. But you had to go, you were always so nosey as a child. Where did you find it?" I asked him.

"I fell into a hole and that's where I discovered it, all sticky and smelly."

"I can't believe you kept that smelly thing all these years, and you carved Bram a horse out of it no less."

"Daina, it was our first adventure together remember? I had to keep it and make something out of it. Although, I feel as though I was meant to find it. Like I was drawn to it."

"Sounds a bit spooky to me Zack" I said. Zack got out of bed and put his night gown on, "Where are you going?" I asked,

"Don't worry, I want to see where the smell is coming from. Stay in bed and rest."

"Oh no, I'm going with you." Zack opened the bedroom door. In the passageway covered by the moonlight rays, stood Langos with his different colour eyes that seemed to be glowing.

"Langos, why are you awake? Do you smell that bad smell too?" And the dog gave a bark. He led us straight to the lounge where the wooden horse was laying. Suddenly, a knock on the kitchen door. I was startled by the knock, Zack comfort me and said, "Its ok my dear, it is a little windy outside tonight." Langos started growling as he walked towards the kitchen.

"Zack! What is that? There it is again." I could see he too was a little startled by the sound.

"Stay right here. I will go see what this knocking is all about." He moved slowly behind Langos towards the kitchen.

As he looked through the back window, I peeped around the kitchen wall to check on them and he turned and said,

"Oh Langos, its fine it's just a loose branch moved by the wind. Daina! It's just a branch that came loose. I will sort it out tomorrow, but that smell." Zack walked towards the lounge. He bent over to pick up the wooden horse but dropped it immediately.

"Oh, damn. That hurt. It felt like I was electrocuted and its painful. That's strange, why can't I pick it up?"

"Really Zack, maybe it was just a cramp or a splinter? That horse must be thrown away before the kids get hurt." When Zack dropped the horse, Langos immediately moved away from it and went to the kitchen.

"What now boy? What is wrong? It's just a stinky piece of wood. I thought dogs like to play with wood? I will get rid of it tomorrow. Come my dear, let us go rest it's still dark out. We need to get more rest before our trip to see Nana." Zack went to the bathroom to check on his hand. He switches the bathroom light on and saw some form of writing appear over his whole right hand, with a burning sensation. Immediately he placed his hand under the running tap water to cool it down. And suddenly, his hand was back to normal, as though nothing had happened. He lifted his hand to the light to see if what he just saw was real, but nothing seems to be wrong with his hand. He thought it best to keep this to himself, because none of it makes sense. And he probably doesn't want me to panic or worry. He switched off the bathroom light and headed for the bedroom. I was fast asleep by the time Zack got into bed. He kissed me goodnight, with thoughts still running through his mind about the writing he saw, he forced himself to go to sleep.

The sun pierced its rays of light through the window and I slowly started opening my eyes. I felt as though someone was watching me. I turned and saw Langos.

"Oh, good morning my boy, do you want to go outside? I hope you didn't make a mess in the house?" and just after I spoke, Zack turned towards me and asked,

"Who are you talking too?" I replied,

"Langos my dear, he is sitting beside the bed." Zack realized through his tiredness, he closed the bedroom door last night and had second thoughts. One of the children must have opened the door, because a dog cannot open the door by himself.

"Okay Daina, since you more awake than I, and he listens to you all the time. Can you take him outside?" Zack started pulling the duvet cover over his head.

"Really Zack? Have you forgotten about our trip today to see Nana? Pat will be here soon."

"Daina, I just need 5 more minutes. I will get up very soon, and I will make sure the boys are up too." Suppose that's good enough, I thought.

"Okay boy, let me get my gown and slippers and we can go outside." I got out of bed and saw my gown and slippers lying next to me.

"Oh boy, you are such a clever dog. Thank you for getting my slippers." Within that moment, I realized that I hung my gown up behind the bedroom door the night before, and my slippers were in the cupboard. That's strange I thought, but perhaps I must be mistaken.

"Okay Langos, let's go outside." Down the passage we go towards the kitchen. I opened the back door and out he ran, but not entirely out of my sight.

"No wind my boy. What a peaceful quiet morning it is." He ran around the backyard sniffing and inspecting every tree, except for the tall skinny tree in the backyard. He slowly stopped running about and stood still in the middle of the backyard. Still standing on the back porch, I wondered what he will do next. Langos started howling, followed by little barks. As though he was communicating with someone.

"Langos!" I shouted, "Come boy get inside! I hope you are done, because I am not standing here for the whole day waiting for you." Langos did his business behind a random bush and came back towards me immediately. While running towards the house, I noticed something move. It was close to that tall skinny tree in the yard and Langos was startled. He stopped and gave a bark.

"Oh boy, why are you barking? It can only be the squirrels my boy, they must be playing or collecting nuts. Let's go inside." I can't help but feel a presence in the backyard. I need to block out my fears because I know it will affect my baby. Langos followed me into the house, just as the kettle stopped boiling.

"Coffee time, and breakfast time for you boy." I reached for the door to close it, and took one last look in the yard. I could have sworn I saw a tree branch move. That's almost impossible because there is no wind. Come to think of it, where are the birds? They usually chirping away at this time of the morning. "Okay, Daina, don't talk yourself into something you're not sure of." I thought to myself silently. The clock shows 6am.

"Okay boy let's start with a nice cup of coffee for me and a bowl of doggie food for you." I started making my coffee and gave Langos some food, which he enjoyed. The doorbell rang, and Langos jumped up immediately.

"That could only be Pat. We are all going on a trip today. And you will meet my great-aunt Nana." I peeped through the front window as Langos stood next to me. I was right, it was Pat. I opened the door.

"Good morning my child, I hope I am not too early." Greeted Pat.

"Oh no Pat, I was just about to call the boys."

"Alright dear. May I come in?"

"Come in Pat, we are almost done and ready to go." Zack shouted from the kitchen. I was pleasantly surprised to see Zack and the boys up, dressed and almost ready to go.

"What is going on?" I said surprised, walking towards the kitchen with Langos and Pat behind me.

"What do you mean my love?" Zack had a boyish grin on his face because he knew exactly what I meant. "I told you I only needed 5 more minutes." The boys were extremely excited, they ran off to finish packing after they greeted Pat.

"Relax and be happy I have everything under control." I looked at Zack with a smile on my face as I responded,

"Thank you, my love. I will try and relax more."

"Boys are you almost done? Did you pack the right clothes, because I am coming to do an inspection?"

"Yes Ma, we are ready for you." The boys shouted from their room. I made my way to the kids' bedroom, while Zack and Pat started packing the road trip snacks.

"Okay Pat, I will get the car ready for us to start packing the suitcases in. I need to make space for Langos in the back."

"I see you getting used to your new dog." Pat said

"Oh yes, but he seems more taken to Daina."

"Well, we will see about that. I predict you will become very good friends." Zack looked at Pat with a smile. He turned towards the door that led to the garage. Zack walked around outside, checking the grounds before we leave. He walked past the kids' window, and overheard me saying,

"Okay, all seems to be packed in. Take your bags to your father so that he may put them in the car. And I will get ready for our trip." Zack smiles and continues his final checks.

I headed for the bedroom to start getting ready, so that we may leave. On my way to the bedroom, I overheard Pat talking to someone in the kitchen. I turned slowly and walked towards the kitchen to see who he was talking too. I saw him talking to Langos, "Boy you better be good on the trip, no outbursts. You know there are eyes and ears everywhere." I walked straight into the kitchen,

"Pat, is everything ok? I couldn't help overhear you, but you are aware that you are talking to a dog. I know he seems very clever but he is after all only a dog or am I mistaken?" I asked.

"Oh no my child, have you forgotten what you witnessed last night? I'm certain that you have not. But say no more, we will discuss this much later." I could feel a warm sensation overcome me as he spoke, and then a sudden burst of calmness.

"I don't understand what I saw Uncle Pat. It is impossible to explain."

"You will understand everything soon enough." Langos walked towards me and put his head under my hand for me to rub him.

"Okay Uncle Pat. I will not utter a word to anyone." I looked at my watch, "Oh look at the time, I still need to dress." I left for the bedroom. Had a shower and got dressed. As soon as I was done, I headed for the lounge where everyone was waiting for me.

"Really Ma, it's already more than an hour." Bram turns to face Pat. "Uncle Pat, why are girls so slow?" he asked.

"Bram you watch it little man, because I will leave you next door."

"Oh no, not that woman, she always wants me to clean her yard. I will be good."

"Let's go family." Zack said. Langos started making his way with the kids and myself towards the car, while Zack locked up.

"Ma, why does Langos act so strange? Like his watching or listening for danger?" Asked Seth.

"It's a dog's instinct to protect, so his looking out for bad people."

"Okay Ma. So, Langos is a good boy and he can have some of my burger later?"

"Yes."

"Everyone is in the car, my dear. Let our journey begin." I said to Zack. The car pulled away from the driveway and Langos turned and looked out of the back window of the 4x4. He saw something moving in the distance and gave a huff. Pat immediately turned and saw the same thing.

"I think it will be a good idea to stay on the highway right through instead of using the dirt road. What are your thoughts?" Pat asked Zack and continued before he could answer, "…also the dirt road has a very rough terrain, we need to consider Daina's condition."

"Okay great thinking Pat." Zack replied in agreeance. "I was actually considering taking the old road, but you're right."

"Okay guys, I am here. I am not invisible; you know and it's called being pregnant not disabled." I responded.

"Sorry my love." Zack said, "we didn't mean it in a bad way, just really considering you. So, highway it is then." When Zack reached the highway on-ramp he made himself comfortable for the long trip.

"How long will it take to get there, Papa?" Bram asked.

"I think about 7 to 8 hours my boy." Zack replied

"Okay Papa. Sounds like a nice adventure."

"Oh yes, my boy. You will see the mountains and the lake we have to cross. Although you might fall asleep."

"No Papa. Please wake me up. I would like to see the lake."

"Alright. I will my boy." We all started settling in for the long journey ahead. Bram sat close to Langos, as he started drifting off, he couldn't help but wonder about the colour of Langos' eyes, and he thought he had to ask.

"Uncle Pat, do you know a lot about dogs?"

"I wouldn't say a lot, but I do know enough. What would you like to know?" Pat turns to look at Bram sitting at the back.

"Well, can a dog's eye colour change overnight? I know it sounds crazy, but I think Langos had black eyes, but now he has colour eyes?" Bram said. I fell asleep during the conversation between Bram and Pat. I started dreaming about walking towards a place I have never seen before, but as a child. I saw an animal; I was not too sure of what type of animal. It was peacefully standing watching me and I had no fear. I felt very calm until I saw a cloud of black fog in the distance moving slowly towards my direction. Immediately I felt scared, and all I wanted to do was run. But I couldn't move, as though I were frozen. As the fog moved closer, I saw Langos running towards me. He jumped into the big cloud of black fog and I wake up. I yelled as I woke, and Zack responded immediately;

"Are you okay? You must've had a bad dream?"

"I'm okay Zack, yes just a silly dream." I replied. As soon as I said those words, I turned to look at Langos and I could see him puffing away like he ran a marathon.

"You okay boy?" I asked Langos.

"Zack, I think he needs to pee and stretch."

"Oh no my love, I just started the cruise control. Really getting into it now."

"Zack, just find a quick spot!" I urged.

"No, there's a garage a mile away. We shouldn't stop along the road just anywhere, it's dangerous." Pat said

"Okay, you're right Pat. But the next stop, okay Zack?"

"Okay my dear, next stop it is." Zack said in agreeance. I started relaxing while watching the children sleep. Pat and Zack kept a good eye on the road while Zack was driving. I turned slightly to look through my window and saw how the sun was slowly rising. I thought silently, it's going to be a beautiful day today. I thought about the questions I want to ask Nana because there was no use asking Pat. He always avoids everything you ask or advises you to ask Nana because she will remember. I looked at Pat and thought, you know more about my life then what you're letting on, but why don't you want to tell me more? I really wonder about my childhood, that's the most important thing on my mind right now, that I want cleared up. And what is it with this big tree that no one is allowed to pass. I haven't even seen this big tree, or have I? I can't remember much before the age of 10 years old. The earliest memory I have, is of a day when I had a funny looking dress on, with no shoes and my feet was muddy and cold, and I felt very tired and sleepy. I then saw Nana and she lifted me up to carry me home. But where was home? I am baffled.

"Uncle Pat, what was my mother's name?" I asked with no hesitation, "Nana never talks about her nor my father." Langos sat up and tried to get me to rub his head but I asked Pat again ignoring Langos.

"Uncle Pat, my parents? What happened to them?"

"Oh, my child, I think Nana should tell you about their life. My memory is not that good anymore, but I do remember you were only a baby when we got you." He said.

"Got me? From whom Uncle Pat?"

"Daina, I don't remember. Nana has a diary she uses for record, and she will explain everything to you once we have settled in."

"First stop everyone, get ready. Who wants to use the restroom and stretch their legs?" Zack said interrupting me before I could ask another question. I started waking the children, while Zack parked the car.

"The sun looks really pretty Ma." Seth said, while staring out the window.

"Sun please stop the car; I need to go to the little boys' room." Bram said.

"Hold on Bram, your father also has to go. So, wait for him." I replied

"I do? Where must I go?" Zack asked

"Zack please just take him to the boys' room. He obviously won't go with me."

"No Papa, I can't go into a girls' bathroom! The girls might see me."

"Hold on little man." Zack parked the car and off the boys went.

"Okay that leaves us." Pat said, "I will take Langos for a walk and meet back soon."

Everyone went their separate ways. Langos was very alert, as though he thought danger was everywhere.

"Okay Langos, what is going on with you? You cannot react to every sound that passes by. Daina senses that there is something different about you. Bram already has questions. Listen, you may think you are normal compared to everyone else, but you are on a different Plain. Here the rules are quite different. You know how important Daina and the child are, their wellbeing is crucial because of their existence. You have to be careful Langos, not to put fear in Daina. I have sensed what follows us and that's why we need to get to our Domain." Pat instructed Langos on their walk. Langos looked at Pat and gave a strong bark showing that he understood everything he said.

"Alright now that that's settled Langos, let's go see if the others are back yet." He said feeling a lot better after their chat. I walked towards the 4x4, while Zack and the boys sat on a bench waiting for me, Pat and Langos.

"Okay family, now that everyone is here, let's go." Zack said and everyone jumped back into the car.

"We have 6 hours to go, hopefully we will reach Nana by lunch time." He said.

"That sounds great!" I replied with enthusiasm.

"You know kids, I'd like to show you a waterfall that breaks into a big lake. Your father and I used to jump from that waterfall into the lake when we were kids." I turned to look at Zack.

"Zack, do you think the children are old enough to take them on the walk?" I asked

"Oh yes my dear, but you will not be able to go with, remember there's a bit of a climb." He responded

"Oh, yes I remember. Okay guys we can go to the lower lake, Pat can show us the way."

"Your mother has snacks for you boys, if you would like some or you could sleep some more, because we still have some distance to cover." The boys nodded their heads in response to Zack. In no time we were back on the road and the boys and I slowly started to relax. Zack pointed out the Mountain of Blufoos, farther on in the distance, covered in a blanket of snow. There was a forest below the mountain, filled with different types of trees as far as the eye could see.

"Look boys, can you see the pathway climbers use to reach the top? Perhaps one day when you're older we will go there."

"Oh yes, Papa that sounds exciting."

"Daina, remember the lake we had our picnic when the boys were a younger?"

"Yes." I said and turned to look through the right window. I could see down the valley, a beautiful big lake flowing through the mountains.

"It's called the Lake Crandel. If I'm not mistaken Zack."

"Yes, it is really beautiful. Look at how dark the water looks from above." The boys turned to look out of the window on the right side of the car, and became excited.

"Look." Bram said pointing his finger to show his brother all the trees down there.

"I can see a boat, look Ma!"

"Yes, we are going to cross over that bridge soon. Can you see it in the distance?"

"Yes." Both responded.

"And can you boys see the mountain with the snow that Papa spoke about earlier?"

"Yes."

"Nana lives close to that mountain."

"That sounds exciting." They seem rather exhausted. I suggested they close their eyes and sleep for a little while. Within an instant, I took my own advice and drifted off to sleep. Pat turned and looked at Langos and saw him sitting straight up. He could sense danger. He needed to do something about it and thought to himself he may need to push time forward to get closer to their boundary of the woods that led into their domain.

"Zack, you look rather exhausted. I'll drive for a while and you can take a break."

"Okay Pat. I only need half an hour, then I will be as good as new." Zack slows down to turn into a small garage nearby to change seats. The rest of the family were sleeping soundly and hadn't noticed that they stopped. Pat mumbled a few words, instantaneously the whole family was fast asleep. Langos looked at the clock and saw it moving. Time sped up. The car was now travelling as fast as the speed of light. The road ahead became one straight line, the trees and green fields around us smudged together to form a horizontal plain. The clouds disappeared into the blueness of the sky as it formed a canvas that filled in everything else. Nothing can be seen with the naked eye at the speed of light, your brain merely filters in images that your mind can comprehend. What a sight indeed. Langos gave a huff at Pat.

"Yes Langos, I can smell them following us. Don't fret, we are crossing the boundary soon and they cannot enter. Daina and the family are safe, calm down. They will wake up soon once we cross the bridge." He said calmly to Langos while everyone else falls deeper into their slumber. Pat crossed the bridge and we all start waking up slowly.

"Oh my, are we here already?" I asked, while wiping the sleep out of my eyes.

"Yes, my child, home sweet home." Pat replies. Zack, who had also just woken up from his deep sleep, looks through his window from the passenger seat and says;

"I thought we were hours away. I must've really been tired. Thank you, Pat, for taking over the driving." We drove up the driveway towards the big house. The different types of bright coloured flowers that bloomed along the driveway always had a way of making me smile. They were breathtakingly beautiful. The tall strong oak tree in the front yard, still has my swing that Uncle Pat made for me all those years ago. The more we drove, the closer we got to Nana's house. It was made of marble stone, with crystal finishers around the windows and doors. It was magnificent and stupendously beautiful, I believe. Her house stood at the end of the driveway on a slight hilltop. It had a massive porch made out of the finest dark wood with a few steps that led to the driveway. Her windows shimmer with colour, each one never the same colour as the other. I used to think it all depended on your mood, but I have since come to learn that it depends on the angle you are looking from. Fascinating indeed. Her rooftop soared higher than any normal house, reaching the perfect point effortlessly, making this house the best in the land. We could see Nana sitting on the porch waiting for us. Nana had thick black curls with grey highlights that appeared silver in the sun. Her skin was as clear as a summer's day and her beauty could never be forgotten. Pat stops and the children jump out to greet Nana. I slowly got out to with the help of Zack. Langos kept a close eye on us the entire time. We started walking towards Nana and the old woman gave such a big smile, filled with joy. She shouted;

"Our princess has come home!" and wrapped her loving arms around me. Within a second, I felt the warmth of love and happiness, but also felt something was amiss. Nana turned towards me and said,

"Yes, my child, I know you have a lot of questions that need answers. But for now, you are safe and everything will be okay." I felt as though I couldn't ask Nana anything, because for some reason I know I will see and understand everything soon enough.

CHAPTER 3

THE AWAKEN

I took a moment to reminisce and take in the view from the porch before going inside. It has been a long while since my last visit and yet nothing has changed. The grass is greener than ever before and it always manages to stay short. I wonder if Nana has a private gardener stashed away somewhere, that probably comes out every other day or two to trim the edges. One may never know. The air smelt filtered and fresh; a lot thinner but also richer. As though there may be gold; fit for your lungs floating in the air. The sun's rays looked like diamonds reflecting off every bit of nature that it could find, leaving you paralyzed in awe of its beauty. The woods in the far distance covered Nana's property like a barricade. I always knew there was something strange about these woods, but I could never put my finger on it. These woods were not like any other, they were calm and tranquil. When viewed from a distance, it seems as though nothing but the finest parts of nature reside in there. The feeling doesn't change, the closer you are, and that's what makes it strange.

"Nothing has changed since I left the house." I mentioned softly to Nana

"Yes, nothing much has change. And now that you are home, everything be better." She responded softly.

"Come my children, let's get you all settled in." Nana showed us inside. The children started running inside the house.

"No running children!" The last thing I need is someone getting hurt, I thought.

"They are exactly like you, when you were a child." She smiled softly with delight in her eyes as she reminisced for a moment. I entered through the door; the staircase that led to the top floor was made of dark yellow wood. The walls were painted in a soft yellow colour. Halfway up the staircase, there was a big window that shimmered with bright colours, depending on how you look at it. The floors had a white marble finish with a long carpet that ran between the wall and the stairway that led to the kitchen. Nana had antique furniture that was perfectly preserved and elegant. And an old clock I called Mr. Ticker, still stood in the corner of the lounge area ticking away. As I looked around, I could see Nana watching me with a smile on her face and I tried to think of more memories of my younger years, but nothing. I turned to Nana, took her hand and said.

"Nana, please tell me about my childhood, I must know more." I could see the truth in her eyes, so there was no denying it. She knows everything I need to know.

"My child, you only just arrived. There's a lot of time to dig up old ghosts, but right now is not that time. We can talk about everything once you have settled in." I looked at Nana and said;

"Okay let me get the children settled, then we can make some lemon juice and talk. Nana do we still have the lemon tree?"

"Oh yes my child. It has been blooming and bearing special lemons for many years."

"Okay then, the kids will really enjoy picking some lemons." I thought it would be a good idea as an activity of some sort for the boys.

"I see you have a new member of the family." Nana called out from across the room.

"Oh Nana, yes sorry. I thought it wouldn't be a problem to bring Langos. The children found him a few days ago. He is really good and won't be a problem."

"No problem my child, he is welcome at our house. He is part of the family since he is with you, but what did you call him?"

"Langos is his name Nana!" I shouted, on the off chance that perhaps Nana may be losing her hearing.

"My child, why are you shouting? I might be getting old, but I'm not going deaf."

"Sorry Nana, maybe I'm a bit tired. I should get some rest."

"Yes, you should." I made my way up the staircase to the boys' room. They were playing with their toys.

"Boys, why aren't you unpacking your clothes?"

"Ma, can't we do it later? We took our pj's out and that should be ok until tomorrow?"

"Okay my boys." I had no energy to argue

I walked towards my old bedroom and started thinking about my past and as I looked around the bedroom, it brought back such good memories. And still, I had so many questions. I made my way to the bed and laid down. Ever since I became a mother, I always wondered about my real parents. What ever happened to them? Nana also told me, 'just remember we love you and your mother and father would've been so proud of you', but what ever happened to them? If they died, where are they buried? Hopefully, I will get the answers I seek once and for all. While I rested, Zack and Pat unpacked the rest of the suitcases from the car. Zack walked into the house when Pat says to him;

"My boy, you go ahead and bring everything inside. I need to give your Nana a big kiss and squeeze hello."

"Oh Pat really, too much information." Pat started laughing and made his way towards the garden where Nana sat.

"Nana my dear, are you okay? You didn't say much on our arrival."

"Yes Pat, I see you took a huge risk today. Amusing yourself with time, what if Daina woke and saw the world flying past at the speed of light? How would you have explained that?"

"My dear, please don't overreact. I had everything under control and I made sure all of them were in a deep sleep, especially Daina."

"But Pat, you know you shouldn't play with time outside of the Plain. You wouldn't want someone woken up before the time." Pat looked at Nana and said,

"We already had a few incidences at their house and on the road. Langos appeared before my arrival."

"What are you saying? Please explain."

"Everything already started, even before I got to Daina."

"How does Daina know Langos' name? I don't understand."

"I told you a long time ago Nana, you were supposed to prepare her for the days that lay ahead. It's going to be very difficult for her to understand the truth. Because you've been hiding everything from her. Something happened with Langos while he was with her. I think she's sensing her true nature now. She's so close to her Plain, so please tell her before it's too late."

"I know what I'm doing, there are rules to follow and they cannot cross into our Domain and the surrounding Plain."

"You really don't listen, they already did. One of the Trimos clans was in Daina's backyard. Lurking around, that's when Langos arrived. He could sense she was in danger. That's why he was awoken and found her." He had a transformation in front of Daina and had to shield her from the Trimos.

"Has Daina said anything or told anyone?"

"No, I believe she has not. Her denial is far greater than her understanding."

"Why didn't you tell me that earlier Pat?"

"Nana, I did. You don't listen, because you're so stubborn. And it has been well over a thousand years."

"I need to speak to Langos immediately Pat, please call him." Pat quickly rushes off to the front porch when Nana called him back and said,

"It's too late, he went into the woods. He will be back later." Pat turned halfway and looked at Nana now standing, and asked.

"Why have you chosen a dog for Langos?"

"Well, just remember a dog is man's best friend my dear." She replied and continued,

"Once Daina is rested, I will have our long overdue chat with her. I am certain that she will have more questions concerning Langos' transformation. I am well aware of the questions she has no doubt prepared for me. What I don't understand is; why would the Trimos react so uncharacteristically? Do you think they wanted to hurt Daina? I truly cannot understand why, and without Langos here, I cannot see the visions he saw. He is too far in the woods, and too close to the big tree. That is the last I saw of him." Nana said with uneasiness in her voice.

"Oh Pat, I don't understand why there is such an imbalance. That's why there is the Law of the Realm. No-one, neither King nor Queen, and none of us would dare break the law. Everyone of Natures Domain, knows the punishment is to be banished to the outer realms, where all evil go. I will need to go to the big tree and set things right. Before the Creators step in and see the imbalance. They have been waiting for this day, all fate is depending on it."

"You have to explain all this to Daina first, before you do anything. She has to understand what is about to happen, because we will have no control if the Creators step in." Pat said to Nana

"Pat, I need to go and see the elder. Please my dear, fetch my coat and staff and keep time in its place for now until I return."

"Now I'm allowed used my gift, but before I was told not too by you."

"You are Father Time; the keeper of time so please do this for me."

"Okay my dear, off you go. I will keep everyone in place until your return."

"Just remember Pat, be careful. Daina might not be affected."

"Don't worry my blossom, I have something special for her. I will put her in a sleeping time loop, she will never know the difference." Pat mumbles some words and time starts slowing down until it eventually stops. I fell into a deeper time sleep.

"Okay my dear it's done, go on now." Nana takes her coat and staff and walks down the pathway towards the woods. Time doesn't affect her, because she is Mother Nature and Pat is Father Time. They are the Balance Keepers of the Realm, created by The Creators. As Nana walked through the woods, she could feel the darkness slowly creeping between the trees. Each step she took turned to ice, wherever the darkness followed. Nature is affected by Nana's emotions; this darkness turned her mood ice cold. A restless wind followed her every step throughout the woods. She walked towards a big oak tree that stood against a hill. Upon arrival she stamped her staff on the ground three times. This is no ordinary staff, it's The Staff of Algara, the Keeper of Nature. The tree awakens from a deep slumber.

"Mother, I can sense why you have woken me."

"Dajeti, Wood Keeper. I have woken you because there is an imbalance in the Realm."

"Mother, my roots grow deep and far beyond the Plain's. There are many outsiders I see. Outsiders who do not know the old ways, and do not want to learn either. Their roots have been poisoned by some of the Trimos clan, and have been woken before the child is born. They are growing stronger Mother. They have moved to the side of the Lady Ciandra from the Trimos clan. She tried to destroy her own family, the Protectors of the Trimos Domain, so that she could fight to become Queen of Athela. Now they are her own prisoners. The Being that could give such a command to the young unrooted must be Lady Ciandra because she has discovered that Daina is the true Princess, and the true Heir of the thrown of the Realm. She carries with her the Child of Light, half human and half nature. I can see the unborn child is a girl, Mother." Dajeti said.

"The Princess will need to take her place, to pass on the crown to the Child of Light. If there is no balance Mother, the Creators will judge and might destroy the Realm." Nana put her hand on the big tree and said; "I feel your pain. I pity man, and nature. I have felt the pain that has been brought to this Realm, since the dawn of days, but there is still hope in the unborn child." Dajeti's leaves start to fall from its branches.

"Mother it's almost time. You need to go. I will call upon Langos." The ground started shaking and a beautiful door opened through the trees' trunk. A bright light appeared with a pathway that led to another place, filled with mountains, rivers and spectacular woods. In the distance, Langos walked towards the doorway.

"You called Wood Keeper?" Langos said. He quickly realized who was standing in front of him.

"Mother, why are you here?" Baffled, he asked. "I am inclined to think that I would only be summoned once the family has settled in. I presume she is safe, since we are in your domain."

"Not quite, it would seem Langos. Pat has told me about the threat you saw while you were with Daina. Langos, what woke you from your deep sleep to find Daina? You were woken too early. I need to see your visions Langos."

"Mother, I was woken up by my Inner Spirit and could sense Daina was in danger. I needed to bring her to your Domain because I am not strong enough yet to protect the Princess on the Plain of Mankind. When I was close to the Princess, I transformed into an older form that allowed me to shield her from the young Trimos clan. That was when Father arrived." Nana had a look of concern on her face.

"What was the Princess' reaction when she saw this happening?"

"I felt a peaceful feeling coming from her and my Inner Spirit was drawn to something I do not know of. That is why when I knew the Princess was safe in your Domain, I had to go to my place of rest because of the amount of energy I used to transform. Mother, I hope there has not been any form of imbalance because of the transformation in front of the Princess on the Plain of Mankind."

"No, my son. Thus far nothing has been revealed to me. But I need to see your visions." Nana looked at Langos, bent down on one knee and put her hand on him and said; "show me your vision." Langos closed his eyes and showed Nana what he could foresee. A few minutes pass and Nana gets up from her bended knee and steps away.

"Langos, what you have shown me, there is only one thing that needs to happen. The time has come for you to take your place in the Realms and become what you were set out to be." Nana spoke firmly and with conviction. Langos seemed a little confused,

"Mother I do not understand my vision, and what you have said is not clear to me."

"My son, do not be weary for you will soon discover your true self-worth."

"I will go back to the house and start preparing for what may come. Langos you need to go find the King Tree spirit and summon him to come to me. Dajeti my old friend. We need to call upon The Protectors of the Plain of Athela. The time for the gathering of ceremony has come. We must prepare for the war that is about to happen in the Plain of Athela. Something lurks in the darkness surrounding Nature." Langos turned and started walking back towards the big tree. He nodded his head and disappeared into the light. Dajeti closed his door and said to Nana,

"I hope the balance can be resorted without war." Nana looks at Dajeti and said,

"My friend, the road ahead might look dark and gloom, but Princess Liara has returned. Not all hope is lost. I will return in one day." And with that said, Nana made her way back home.

Nana walked through the woods, still feeling that coldness surround her. Once she entered the boundaries of her house, it suddenly disappears. Nana walked up to her porch and found Pat sitting eagerly waiting her return.

"My dear, what happened?" he asked.

"Well, it is just as I have predicted many years ago. If the darkness that is lurking around Athela is not destroyed before the Child of Light is born, the full scale of the imbalance will be revealed to the Creators. It must be restored. I do not have the power nor the ability to keep the Vail in place." Pat questioned, "What do you mean by the Vail?"

"The Vail is what keeps the two Plain's separate from each other. Once the Vail has been lifted, the world kept within worlds, which is the Plain of Athela, will be revealed to the Plain of Mankind. The two Plains are connected through the Princess and Zack, which is forbidden by the Creators. That is why the Vail must remain intact. The Creators know that if another is born from two separate Plains, they will possess a power far beyond their control. Despite the goodness that was created, with no hesitation they will destroy the full Realm of Ekna; as it is known to the Athelians and Earth as it is known to Mankind."

"You know what you have to do, its time." Nana took her coat off and said, "Father Time, let time be. Bring back reality." And with her words spoken, Pat mumbles and snaps his fingers, and the clock started ticking once more. They could hear the children laughing and Zack coughing but I remained quiet. Pat made his way to my room, to check on me. While Nana made her way to the kitchen. I called out to the boys to behave, and Pat immediately stopped. Turned around and made his way back to Nana in the kitchen.

"All is well. Everyone is back to normal." Nana gave a smile and said,

"I see you haven't lost your touch." Pat smiled and made his way back to the porch. Nana walked towards the hallway and shouted, "Zack, how about you and the boys go fishing?" Immediately the boys came running down the stairs,

"Yes Nana. That will be fun." Zack and I made our way to the kitchen where we found Nana talking to the boys.

"That's a great idea." Zack responded. He walked past Pat sitting on the porch and asked if he would join them. Pat politely turned down the offer. As I greeted the boys and told them to have fun, I noticed Langos was nowhere to be found.

"Where is Langos?" I asked Nana

"His playing with the neighbour's dog." Pat shouted from outside. But I wondered if that were true. Pat got up from the porch and walked towards the kitchen.

"Do you ladies fancy a stroll in the woods?"

"Oh yes. That will be lovely." I said thinking this will be my opportunity to get some answers from Nana.

"Off you go ladies, and enjoy." Pat said. Nana started making her way to the porch with me right on her heels.

"Nana will you tell me what I need to know?" She stopped and turned around to look at me.

"All will be revealed my child, just have patience. Fetch your Nana her walking staff." I quickly grabbed the staff and gave it to Nana. We walked down a walkway to the edge of the path that led into the woods. Nana stopped and said,

"When we pass this tree, do not look back." Baffled I said,

"Yes Nana, but I don't understand." Nana took my arm and said, "My child, all your questions will be answered. But that is my rule." I nodded my head and responded,

"Yes, I promise I will not look back." Nana took her staff and knocked it once on the ground. Nana and I walked into the woods called, The Woods of Calm. I felt a bit frighten at first, and I could feel the baby kicking. An unsettled feeling overwhelmed me.

"I think this is far enough." I insisted to Nana. Out of nowhere, Langos appeared. I felt slightly confused but calm when I saw Langos. Even though I could not help thinking about what I saw.

"Come boy, walk with us." Nana suggested and without delay, I felt relieved and calm. We started making our way towards the Big tree. When Nana turned onto another path towards the lake where I use to play as a child. Nana found a cozy spot overlooking the beautiful lake, as far as the eye could see.

"Oh Nana, I remember this place. What wonderful memories. Including the Bingjie water monster that Pat use to tell us about and warned us not to go further down the lake, because he will catch us." We burst out into laughter.

"Oh that Pat, he always had a way to tell a story. Silly old fool." she laughed, "Daina, do you still intrigued by storytelling?" she asked.

"Well I think I'm a bit too old for stories Nana, but what is the story about?"

"It's called The Journey of the Forgotten Kahul." This should be interesting I thought, and I made myself comfortable.

"Once upon a time, there was nothing and the Universe was empty, no life at all. But then a light appeared where there was only darkness and with that light, creation was born into some form of energy. The energy was a type of source. A form of ability was created through the light of the universe. The light split into many spheres of energy sources. Only six remained and from that energy, there were Beings created, known as The Creators." I sat and listened to Nana word for word ever so attentively while enjoying her story. Langos kept a watchful eye on the surrounding area. I looked at Langos and said, "this is such an interesting story boy, wish you could understand," and with that said, Langos gave a little bark as though he may have said yes. Nana looked at Langos and said to me, "I think he does understand my child,"

"Okay Nana, let's continue please."

"Alright, where was I? Oh yes, The Creators. Well, the Creators are Beings that created life in different Realms, and we are part of those Realms. There are four Realms similar to our world but one Realm is called the Outer Realm."

"Really?" I said interrupting Nana, "What is that?"

"I will explain, in due time. In some of the Realms there are different Plains that have life forms."

"Nana, now I'm confused. Creators? Realms and Plains? What next? Kings? Fairies and Princesses?"

"Daina, please my child, try to listen and understand. Thereafter I will tell you about your parents and your upbringing."

"Oh Nana, please just tell me about them."

"No! I will tell you everything before we leave this place."

"Alright, I will listen." And Nana continued.

"This special tale I am about to tell you, is about a Realm that forms part of two Plains. Mankind and Nature. There is a balance that must be kept. The Creators decided to create two lesser Beings called the Yungnas; Father Time and Mother Nature, to keep the balance in the Realm. Once they were created, life as you now know it was born. This forms part of something you will soon come to understand. Once there lived a King and Queen that ruled the Kingdom of Athela. The Kingdom consisted of three Domains; Famos, Trimos and the water city called Onasia. All three Domains completed the Plain of Athela. Their palace stood high up on the Domain of Famos and the people of Athela were called Athelians. They had a beautiful daughter named Princess Liaana. She was a curious little girl and both her parents and her people loved her very much. As she grew older both her parents had passed on. She became Queen of the Kingdom, but she fell in love with Dramos. He was from the Trimos Domain, Dramos is the eldest son of Protector Lickso and Lady Savala. They are the protectors of the Domain of Trimos. They had three children, one daughter named Ciandra and two sons named Acoma and Dramos. The Creators had forbidden any Being from another Domain to become as one. And the punishment was just. If this should ever occur, they will be banished to the outer Realm, where Evil dwells. Everyone in the Realm heard tales of the Outer Realm, and were frightened by it. No one would ever dare to speak of these tales in passing, afraid that they may be punished by the Creators. Queen Liaana and Dramos did not much care about the rules, because love knows no boundaries. The pair fell in love and Liaana was with child. The Creators discovered the deception, and just before they were banished to the Outer Realm, Liaana gave birth to a beautiful baby girl. The Creators were unaware of the child, because she was taken by Mother Nature and Father Time into the Plain of Mankind. The child was shielded from the Creators, by The Keepers of the Realm and the Source. The child grew up as normal as could be. Nothing was explained to her about her life as a young child, because if the Creators received word that the child lives, they will banish the child and the Realm will become imbalanced. The Creators will destroy that which they have created, and all hope will be lost."

"What happened next Nana?" intrigued I asked

"Well, the child grew up into a beautiful woman, and had a family of her own. She met her husband and they had two wonderful children. She was expecting another, and very happy. They got themselves a dog and went to visit her family for a holiday."

"That sounds strangely familiar Nana. As though you were talking about me and my family?" I said while unconsciously staring into the abyss before continuing.

"Why am I so silly, it's just a story." Frantically trying to calm myself down without showing Nana my anxiety.

"Nana? It is just a story? Is it not?" I asked, afraid to hear the answer.

"You wanted to know your story, did you not? And you wanted to know more about yourself, did you not?"

"Nana, now you're scaring me, what is going on?"

"Daina. The child I told you about in the story is you. Your birth name given to you by your parents is Liara. You are the daughter of Queen Liaana from the Famos Domain and Dramos from the Trimos Domain. You are Princess Liara, true Heir to the Throne of Athela. And destined to become the Queen of the Realm."

"What? Oh no, you must have the wrong person, how can this be?" I said with every ounce in my body covered in denial.

"We hid the truth about your past from you and your parents wish for you, that someday you will be able to bring balance back to the Realm. And when the prophecy is fulfilled, there might be a way to return both your parents from the Outer Realm."

"Nana this is too much for me. I need to go home, back to reality. I think that lemon juice might have gone to your head or it's definitely something else." I got up in a panic.

"Calm down my dear, this will take time but you will see. Soon enough your memories will return." I looked at Langos and said, "And who might you be? King of the dogs? I know you are not what you seem to be, I do remember everything I saw back at home. This stuff is crazy." Langos looked at me without a bark or sound.

"Daina, within four days you will give birth to a beautiful baby girl."

"What? How do you know that?" The old woman takes her hand and places it on my tummy and said, "She will reveal herself to you very soon. I have foreseen her destiny. She is the Child of Light. She bears the mark. Fortunately, the future is never cast in stone, anything can disrupt the path of time that you need to take." Nana turned to look at Langos,

"It's time Langos we must go, Daina needs to rest. I can tell she grows weary." I am bewildered by this story about my past, I cannot seem to grasp the concept fast enough. I took Nana's arm and slowly walked back to the house.

"Nana, is this a dream or a nightmare? I really would like to wake up now." Nana smiled and spoke.

"Once we return back to the house, say nothing to no one. I will make you a very special cup of tea. This will open your senses. It will be good for the baby."

"Nana she's been very quiet. No kicking or fussing. I can't believe I'm having a girl; it will be so fantastic if it is a girl. I always wanted my own little me. Nana, are you sure you not making these stories up?"

"My child, after your tea, you will rest. We will speak of this again in the evening." While walking back to the house with Nana, Langos is on high alert and keeps a look out for any movement. Nana stopped, looked around and said,

"Langos don't worry, they will not dare enter this domain. Remember it is protected by the Shield of Ringmos. Did you summon the Tree Spirit King?" Nana asked

Langos answered in a human voice,

"Yes Mother, the King will appear before the sun sets over the last tree in the valley."

"Oh, my hat! Nana a talking dog! He can speak!" With that said, I passed out.

"Oh Mother, what have I done?" Langos asked frightened to know the answer.

"No my child, it needed to happen. Let's get her to the house. Pat will carry her to the room." Pat was on the porch awaiting our return when he saw what had happened to me and made his way down to help us. He stopped time in the hopes of not wanting to reveal anything to Zack or the kids, and carried me to the room to rest. As Pat laid me down on my bed, I woke up and looked at him baffled.

"How did I get here?"

"You walked here. You then asked me to help you up the stairs so that you may lay down. Don't you remember?" Asked Pat.

"Not really Pat, where is Nana?"

"Nana is making us tea in the kitchen. I will bring you some shortly, for now you need to rest my child."

"Okay will do. Today was a bit of a strange day for me." And just then I remembered Nana's words. "Do not tell anyone." Immediately I said to Pat, "Yes, strange but nice to see the lake from when I was a child. For now, I definitely need to rest."

"Yes rest. When you wake, I will bring you your tea. The boys will be back later." As Pat leaves the room, I couldn't help thinking of what Nana told me. Soon after, I felt this warm calm feeling overcome me and I quickly drifted away. Pat made his way down the stairs towards the kitchen to speak to Nana.

"How did things go?" Slowly sitting down at the kitchen table, he asked.

"Well, I told her a story in a way all parents tell their children about the beginning of time. She took it well. She is definitely a child of royalty. Stubborn, willful and curious. The energy of light I felt coming from her is very powerful. To control it, she must want to will the power. The energy of the unborn baby is so pure and so strong. I have never felt anything like it before." Nana took the kettle off the stove before continuing.

"She will need to be prepared for her unborn child's abilities, including her own. I hope she will understand that we needed to suppress her capabilities, to avoid the Creators finding out about her. They would banish her and punish us all. I have a lot of work to do for these next few days to prepare her for the ceremony. Langos summoned the Tree Spirit King and Daina heard Langos speak. All I can say is, she was flabbergasted." Pat turned towards Langos and asked, "What do you say about that? Why did you do that? Giving the poor girl a fright." Nana turned and responded,

"No Pat, she needed to know. She always knew there was something about him. She will get over it soon. Take this cup of tea to her so she can start opening her mind and relax knowing she's home." Pat takes the cup of tea from Nana and headed up the stairs towards my bedroom. He knocks on the door and enters.

"Oh, thank you Pat for bringing my tea. I really needed one." I started drinking my tea. But just before I could finish it, I started feeling sleepy. Pat made his way to the kitchen and as he walked in, he heard the boys coming down the passage talking and joking around.

"Boys, have you caught a nice fish to cook for supper?" asked Nana

"Oh Nana, the fish didn't want to bite. I think Papa's singing scared them away." Said Bram, and everyone laughed.

"Okay Bram, tomorrow I will take you to a place where all the big fish are." Pat said, "but for now you and your brother go wash up."

"Do we have to Uncle Pat? Can't we play a bit with Langos, please?"

"Okay, but just for another half hour. Then wash time. Please play quietly, your mother had a tiresome day and she's resting." Nana said.

"Is she okay?" Zack asked Nana.

"Oh yes my child. We had a really exciting day with a pleasant walk, she's just a little tired." Zack gives off a heavy sigh of relief and told the boys to go outside and play quietly. The boys made their way out the backdoor with Langos behind them.

"You know Nana, that's a really strange dog. I swear he understands everything we're talking about."

"Oh my child, you just have a very clever and special dog that loves the family very much. Including you." Nana said.

"Really? Then why does he only listen to Daina and the kids?"

"He's a little stubborn, that's all." Pat looked at Nana and started laughing before saying,

"Zack his only a dog, and you still have to gain his trust."

"Maybe you're right Pat, I will try. Well, I'll go check on my better half and get ready for supper." Zack left the kitchen to check on me. He made his way towards the room, slowly tip toeing making sure not to wake me. He peeped in the room and saw me sleeping peacefully. He entered and walked towards the bathroom to take a shower. He couldn't help but stand in the middle of the room to watch me sleep, as though he was seeing me for the first time. He thought to himself, 'what a lucky man I am, to have such a beautiful wife and kids. I am are very excited to meet our new edition.' In that moment he thought, 'what if it's a boy?' 'what do we name him?' 'but what if it's a girl? Oh my, a girl. We will definitely home school her. No one will come close to my daughter or I can always send Langos with her to school to protect her,' with that said, he starts giggling. I woke up from the sounds of his giggles and said,

"Hello you, Mr Giggle. What is tickling you?" He turned and said, "Oh sorry my love. I didn't mean to wake you, please go back to sleep. I am going to shower, so you may continue resting." And he made his way into the bathroom still feeling giggly. I turned to rub my tummy while looking towards the window.

"So little one, I hope you are as excited as I am to meet you?" I got a sudden sense of happiness and felt warmth all over my whole body. "Little one was that you?" And I could see a handprint appearing on the side of my belly for the first time. I could have sworn the baby gave me an answer.

"Alright. So tell me, are you a girl or boy?" Immediately the colour pink appeared in my mind. I was startled by this.

"You can hear and understand me?" And out of nowhere I could hear a faint voice saying,

"Yes Mamma, I am your daughter." I jumped out of the bed and rushed towards the kitchen.

"Nana, what is happening to me?" Pat turned towards me to calm me and sat me down.

"Nana, please tell me?!"

"Pat, you know what to do." Pat mumbled some words and the clock stopped. I started breathing heavily.

"Keep calm my child, slow down and take small breaths." Nana said as she took me by the hand and led me towards the back yard. I saw my children frozen in time, including everything that surrounded them. Except Langos, as he made his way towards us.

"What is going on Nana?"

"Liara, that is your given name. I told you the story about the different Kingdoms and the Creators. Everything I have told you is true. I need you to listen carefully. You and your unborn child are in grave danger. You need to keep calm so that you may open your mind and heart. Try to think back to the day you were born. The moment you opened your eyes for the first time."

"Nana really? How is that even possible? No one can remember as far back as their birth."

"You were a very special baby, just like your unborn child. She has the ability to talk to you. As did you with your mother. That is why she can reach out to you, like you did with your mother. You come from a gifted line of Royalty. That is why both of you are very special and unique and we must protect you at all costs."

"Nana, why could I not speak to or sense the boys?"

"My child, your ability only came to light because you are having a girl. The Universe created light and that is what a female represents. Light gives life and only a woman can be the vessel of life, and the Queen of The Realm. If you take your place, you can pass your Kingdom to your daughter and she will be the heir to your Throne, because she is the Child of Light."

"Nana, why do you keep calling her the Child of Light? I am rather confused and a little frightened."

"There is no need to be frightened about anything. The Child of Light is a Being that was created from both Plains. The Plain of Athela, that is where you are from and Plain of Mankind, where Zack is from. Both you and Zack have created a baby that is forbidden in the eyes of the Creators. She will possess pure power, much greater than the creators and that is why it is forbidden. What I know and understand about the Creators, is that if something exists that they cannot control, they will banish or destroy it. They will destroy the Child of Light because of the power she will possess that they will have no control over. Your child has abilities no other Being, or human has ever seen. Open your mind, so that she may show you her ability, and her stubborn ways, just like you. She has gifts you cannot fathom. But only if she fulfils her destiny. I have summoned the Tree spirit King, to shed light and wisdom on the matter."

"Nana, what is a Tree Spirit King?"

"He is the Spirit of all the trees in the world. If one tree dies, he gives life to another in the form of a flower that blooms or the birth of a new tree. He is wise and good. He will advise on certain visions that are unavailable to me, because of a dark fog I see before me."

"Nana, I had the exact same dream and Langos was there too, trying to protect me. What is going on? I believe everything is true and that frightens me, I worry about what lies ahead for all of us."

"You needn't worry because you have all of us to protect you and your unborn child." Pat interrupted.

"Uncle Pat, what about Zack and the boys? What will happen to them? Please tell me, because this cannot be about me and my unborn baby alone. I have my husband and sons to worry about too and they are my life."

"Everything will be alright. I have already made provisions for them. They will be put in a deep sleep and Langos will be able to shield them from everyone. Including the Creators, until our return." Pat assured me as best as he could. "I cannot stop time when we head off on our journey, it will affect the balance between the Plain of Athela and the Plain of Mankind. Everything must be normal and natural on our journey to Athela."

"I really don't know how to process everything, because it's a lot at this moment." And with that said, I felt a kick and a turn from my baby. "Oh little one, are you hungry or just confused as I am?"

"Okay, I am a very open-minded person and understand the situation we are all in right now. And I will not back down from a fight, no matter what comes my way. But how and when would we know to start with everything Nana?" I asked.

"You will know soon enough." Nana turned to Pat and said, "Please forward time close to supper my dear, so that Daina can go and prepare herself." Pat mumbles his words and time moves forward and I made my way to the bedroom where I found Zack, looking through the window dressed and ready.

"My love, Nana said it's almost time for supper. I'm just going to wash up. Please call the boys to get ready." I asked.

"No problem my dear." He responded and left to check on the boys. As he left the room, he heard the boys make their way to their bedroom.

"Boys you just in time, please get ready for supper."

"Okay Papa." The boys replied, and into their room they go.

Thirty minutes pass and Nana calls everyone, "Supper is ready!" The boys rushed to the kitchen. Ready and clean for supper. While getting dressed, I noticed Zack walked back towards the window he was staring out of before. He had this concerned and sad look on his face. I couldn't help but ask, what was wrong? He turned to face me and said,

"Nothing my dear."

"Oh no Zack, I know when you're lying, please tell me."

"I can feel, something is coming Daina. But I don't know what it is."

"Well it could be the birth of our new child my love, what do you think?"

"Yes, I think it must be that, you have always been so wise." I sat down to brush my hair. Zack still looking out the window, swears to himself that he just saw something moving through the trees. Impossible if there is no wind, he thought. He was not startled by this, he told himself it's only his imagination. He looked at me and said, "You ready?" I turned and said,

"Yes my love, let's go eat." We made our way to the kitchen and sat down at the table, where everyone was waiting. Nana sat after she dished up the food.

"Alright everyone. I just would like to say, I am so happy that I have my family here and its almost time to celebrate someone's birthday, so let's eat." Bram looked at Nana and said,

"Nana have you prayed?"

"Yes my child. A prayer can be prayed by anyone in their own way through thanks giving.

"Oh okay." Said Bram "I like that, so can we eat now, I'm hungry." While the sun was setting, I had a vision. I looked at Nana, as we both saw who was coming up the pathway. Nana turned to look at Pat and he immediately got up, mumbled his words and time stopped.

"Nana, is that who I think it is?"

"Yes my child, no need to fear."

"Easy for you to say. I don't know what I am going to see."

"My child you don't have to worry, you will see what you are meant to see." Nana got up and called me to join her. Langos is right by my side as always. We made our way to the porch, and I see a tall bright figure standing along the porch steps, with long arms and legs that glowed. But there was no face. Strange I thought.

"Greetings Tree Spirit King, thank you for accepting my invitation. I know it has been a long journey for you." Nana said. I thought to myself, how long is long? Where does this figure come from? Perhaps from the other side of the world? I saw humour in that but decided not to let it show. The Tree spirit turned towards me and said in plain English,

"Yes my Queen, my Spirit is spread all around the Plain. And it does take time for me to return as one, to be able to visit you and Mother." Astonished I asked,

"How did you know what I was thinking?" He replied, "I heard your thoughts. And I can see and feel everything in this Realm that was created by the Creators. I am the Spirit of Nature, an ability that was gifted to me by Mother. I have seen your unborn child my Queen and she is the hope of life. I have come today to pledge my loyalty to my Queen and the Child of Light."

"Mother." He turned to Nana, "The pathway through the Wood Keeper to The Plain of Athela is too dangerous. I have seen the young Trimos planning their attack when the Queen returns on that pathway. Dajeti has blocked their way with the Shield of Ringmos to prevent them from entering this Plain. Ciandra has taken Protector Lickso and her brother Acoma prisoner and Lady Savala is in a deep sleep created by her own daughter. Ciandra wants to attack Famos, to take over the Kingdom as Queen of all. The Keepers of Famos have taken up arms to protect the Kingdom, because a great war is coming. Time is running out, Mother. We must act quickly before the Creators step in and destroy this Realm. The Royal Keeper of Famos, Prince Thelon has called upon the Protectors of Athela, because Princess Olia has foreseen a battle in a vision. There is yet another path that leads into the Palace of Famos, but it will be dangerous, because it is full of darkness and the pathway leads through the Bingjie's domain." I looked at Nana and asked, "What is a Bingjie?"

"My child, the stories Pat told you were true. The Bingjie resides deep within the darkness of the lake and does not enter the world above. Unless the Creators are woken."

"Nana that sounds dangerous and absurd. I cannot swim and we are expected to travel along a lake that is home to a monster?"

"Oh no, my child. Not alongside, we will have to go through the water beneath. This will prevent the Creators from seeing us enter the world of the Moeks."

"Who are the Moeks Nana?" I asked, but before Nana could answer, the Tree spirit looked at me and said,

"My Queen, you needn't fear. With your gifts, you will know when to use it. My Queen, Mother, Father and Shield, I have been called upon by you. With a whisper of words, you may call upon me again at any moment to return, when danger is near." In saying that the Tree Spirit King drifted away. I looked at Nana and asked, "Who is the Prince and Princess the Tree Spirit spoke of?"

"Prince Thelon is your cousin and while there is no Queen to rule Althela, the Protectors have been placed next in line; royal blood descendants only. To protect the Kingdom until the true Heir returns. Princess Olia is the daughter of Prince Thelon and she is your first cousin once removed and has the gift of sight." Olia is part of my generation, which makes her my first cousin once removed. The appropriate term to address Olia would be to call her my niece, I will address her has such.

"Well Nana, this is really a lot to digest. There's also the Moeks and this Bingjie. What and who are they? Please explain it." I said, looking at Nana genuinely intrigued.

"I think it best we make our way back inside and sit down to talk once supper is done." We did just that. Moments just before everyone finished their supper, there was a knock on the back door. Silence filled the room before Nana asked Pat to open the door.

"Please do go open, we have a surprise at the door for Daina." Pat slowly got up and smiled at Nana knowing who was at the door.

"Nana, who can that be?" I asked. Zack looked around to see where Langos was, but he was nowhere to be found.

"Daina, where is our so-called guard dog?" Nana looked at Zack and said,

"He went outside to do what all dogs do." Pat opened the door. A beautiful girl was waiting on the other side of that door. She had dark red hair with brown eyes. Her features were very similar to mine, except the red hair, I had pitch black hair with a soft curl.

"Greetings to everyone." She said. It was Princess Olia. Princess Olia walked into the kitchen with Langos right behind her.

"What kind of a guard dog are you? Allowing anyone to knock on the door." Zack told Langos. Nana turned to him and said,

"Oh no child, this is not just anyone. She is Daina's first cousin once removed, Olia. And I was expecting her."

"Oh sorry about that Nana, please accept my apology Olia. I am Zack." Olia turned towards Zack and said,

"I know who you are. You have handsome strong sons." She replied. Bram immediately spoke out and said,

"I like her. Ma, you never told us we had an Aunt? That's so fantastic!" Pat led Olia to a chair to have a seat.

"Is it not time for both of you to go wash and get ready for bed? Remember the fishing spot I told you about? We will need to leave very early tomorrow morning." Pat told the boys and immediately they jumped up and said,

"Thank you for supper, it was nice to meet you Aunt Olia." And off they ran, excited for the next day. Pat cleared the table while Nana sat looking at me.

"Olia? So, you're my long-lost niece that I wasn't entirely aware of until now." I had Zack in my peripheral view, knowing he is unaware of everything I have just learnt about my origin story, I felt quite out of place.

"Uncle Pat? Are you very busy with your time?" Zack turned towards Olia, about to ask her a question when Pat mumbles his words and time stops.

"Nana, Zack will freak out if he hears about my origin story. And now with your visit Olia, it will be very confusing to him, as it is for me at this moment."

"Keep calm my Queen, I am fully aware of everything. I had to come and speak to Mother, as well as you. One wrongful decision can cause the Realm to be destroyed by the Creators and no Athelian can face the Bingjie." Explained Princess Olia.

"I do not understand what you are saying, there must be a way past the Bingjie. For the Shield to find the pathway into the Palace?" Nana said.

"Mother, in the old books of Athela, I have read why the Bingjie were created. It is filled with darkness and feeds off the outer Realm of Evil. It's the destroyer of Realms. Once the Bingjie is woken, no being is safe from its power. It draws your life to extinction. If that happens, the Creators will awake. And if they awake, they will see the imbalance. Everything that is forbidden and the Realm will be no more. The Creators will use the Bingjie to destroy this Realm Mother." Princess Olia explained.

"My child, what does the book say about safe passage through the domain of the Bingjie?"

"Mother, only a pure of heart with no fear and courage can face the Bingjie. That person must come from a bloodline of the gifted. Not from our Plain, but the Plain of Mankind." Nana turned to look at Zack, still frozen in time and said,

"Zack is the one the book had foretold. I can sense his gift, that lays deep within him and that is why he was drawn to you Daina. Since childhood, both your paths were written in the book of the Forgotten Touch. This book was shielded from the Creators centuries ago, before the moons turned into one moon." She said to me

"My child, how did you come across this book?" she asked Princess Olia.

"Well Mother, my Inner Spirit Keeper guided me to the book after Langos was woken and sensed that danger was laying ahead. I had a vision of the Trimos and informed my father Prince Thelon to prepare. I made my way to The Wood Keeper before the Shield was called upon to block the pathway that prevents any being from entering or leaving Athela. Dajeti gave me safe passage to bring my message before my vision came to light. But as you know Mother, nothing is cast in stone yet and it is in the hands of the forgotten one to walk the path of destiny." I sat quietly, listening to everyone speak. I couldn't help but stare at Zack, wondering how he will handle everything once Nana explains it to him. Nana turned to face me and said,

"No my child, you will explain to him in your own words and emotions. Only you have the ability."

"What? Nana you too? Reading my thoughts, well that's not very nice."

"What must I do?" I asked. Princess Olia looked at me and said,

"My Queen, you and your family share so much love. Use your ability to explain to Zack and he will understand. I sense he will accept you as you are. For you are the true Heir to the Throne of Athela and both you and Zack created a child, half Nature and half Mankind, the Child of light. She who brings hope and light to all Beings." I sat back; I felt the baby turning.

"The child is awake and can hear our thoughts and our spoken words. She is almost ready to be revealed into the light of the Realm."

"Daina, please speak to her. You can do so through your thoughts; she will understand you. Your bond is virtually indestructible." Nana said.

"I don't know what to say. This is too much for me. I have learnt I am destined to be Queen, and my child and I are gifted. And my husband must defeat the Bingjie, whatever that is." My voice was shaky and displeasing.

"My child, I think you need to rest. Focus your thoughts on the best way to explain all this to Zack." Nana suggested.

"Pat, it's time for you to let time be." Pat mumbles his words. Zack slowly comes out of his stillness. Zack continued talking to Olia, asking her where was she from. She replied, "A place very close to here." She got up.

"It's getting late, I need to rest." Pat got up and said,

"I will show you your room my child." Zack still looking rather baffled by her not-so-clear answer, replied

"Ok, goodnight then. Perhaps tomorrow we can catch up." Olia greets everyone goodnight and off she went with Pat.

"Daina, she looks nice. You should chat more to her tomorrow about your family history. Since Nana might not remember everything." Zack said.

"Yes my love I will do so. But I think it is time to check on the boys and get ready for bed."

"Goodnight to all." Zack and I greeted before heading to our room.

Nana was sitting in the kitchen with Langos, "Well I think it's going to be a long few days and nights ahead of us. We still have to prepare for what lies ahead." Langos looked at Nana and just nodded his head. Pat walked in shortly after.

"Let's settle in for the evening Pat." Nana and Pat slowly made their way to their bedroom, while Langos stayed and settled in the kitchen to keep watch.

As the evening turned to morning, Olia wakes early and joins Langos in the kitchen. Nana and Pat walked in soon after.

"Good morning everyone." Pat said, as he walked towards the backdoor to sit on the back porch. Langos got up to join him, while Nana started making the morning coffee. Pat and Langos sat outside on the porch, enjoying the morning breeze when they hear a soft cough coming from the top window of our room. Pat turned towards Langos and showed him not to speak. While in the kitchen, Nana pours the hot water for coffee and sat down looking very perturbed. Olia realizes that Nana seemed a bit bleak and tired.

"Mother, what troubles you?"

"Oh my child, I feel very tired. Not sure why." And with that said Langos rushed into the kitchen from the back porch, looking at Nana as though something were coming.

"What's wrong Langos?" and as she spoke, he turned and rushed out the back door towards the woods, as though he were chasing something.

"Langos!" Nana shouted. Pat jumped up and rushed into the kitchen from the back porch trying to find out what all the shouting was about. Nana rushed to the door and saw Langos disappear into the woods.

"Something bad is happening. We need to go see Dajeti immediately Mother." Princess Olia said with terror in her voice. As Pat rushed into the kitchen, Nana instructed him;

"Pat please check on Daina and the family. I need to go with the Princess." He looked at Nana and said, "Alright, go and I will make sure everyone stays safe." Nana took her shawl and staff and they both made their way towards the woods. Pat slowly made his way quietly up the stairs to check on the family. The boys were still fast asleep, as were Daina and Zack. Pat made his way back to the porch where he sat and waited for Nana's return. Nana walked quickly and Olia followed her. Nana stopped and looked at Olia and said,

"My child, I fear the worst is about to happen."

"Mother, I cannot see anything. I have not yet had visions of any sort pertaining to the path that we walk now."

"Dajeti is in pain. I can feel it." Nana started walking faster and came upon the Wood Keeper. Langos was sitting in front of him.

"Langos! What do you sense?"

"Mother, it's Ciandra. She is looking for a pathway that leads to the Bingjie, to wake him to join her in her battle that lies ahead."

"No! Langos that is impossible." Nana said

"No Mother, during the time when the Creators made our Realm, the Bingjie was created too. It was enslaved by the Creators to do their bidding when it was called upon. During the centuries, there was a Trimos Seer that found an object, hidden in the resting place of one of the Creators. It is said, that when you wield that object the Bingjie will obey your command."

"What object?" Nana asked

"Well Mother, it's called the Kahul of Darkness." Olia questioned Langos.

"Why have you not told us about that which you speak of Langos?"

"I cannot explain why Princess. I remembered this only now. It came to me once I felt Dajeti's pain. I could see the times past and the object was revealed to me."

"Dajeti my old friend, do you have any knowledge of this object?" Asked Nana

"Yes Mother. However, I believe the object was lost during the times past. It was never spoken of again. Protector Lickso punished the Trimos Seer for what he has done and banished him to the Pits of Dwelling where there's no return. The item was lost as Langos says, during the times before and never seen again."

"Dajeti, is it possible that Ciandra could find the object with her father's knowledge?" Nana asked.

"No, only the most powerful Seer and the Bingjie itself can reveal the place where the object is hidden." He said. Langos looked at Princess Olia and said,

"My Princess, you have the gift of sight…"

"No Langos, I cannot open my ability to seek such a dangerous object. It has dark powers and the Bingjie will sense the seer that seeks it. It is too dangerous for me." Nana responded to Langos.

"We need to find the Kahul of Darkness before Ciandra does. Zack might not be strong enough to face the Bingjie if Ciandra wields the object."

"Dajeti my friend, give me pathway into your light so I can heal you from within. With my Light, you will feel no more pain and will be healed and protected from the darkness that might be revealed." Langos said.

"Langos, please be careful my child." Nana said.

"Worry not Mother, for I will restore Dajeti and will return before days end."

"Please Mother, return to your home to rest. Langos will return soon." Dajeti reassured Nana. Princess Olia took Nana's hand and off they went, back home.

As they crossed the boundary of the pathway that led to the woods, they could see Pat sitting on the porch anxiously waiting their return. He got up as soon as he saw them and made his way towards them.

"Nana, are you okay my dear? Please come and rest a while, before we start our morning with the family." Pat suggested.

"I'm afraid I cannot. We have much to talk about. We need to plan the path we have to follow. There is much more danger than what we anticipated. We need to call upon the Tree spirit King for help. Olia my child, please summon the Tree spirit King, I am too weak at this moment and we urgently need him."

"My dear, please you need to rest before making any decisions, let alone help. Rest, I will make you some tea. We will discuss everything else later."

"Pat, where is Daina and the family?"

"They are at the little river to catch fish," Pat laughs,

"Invisible fish my dear."

"Oh Pat, that's a terrible thing you have done." Nana said.

"Bram will catch a few fish. But soon after, they will disappear. That should keep them all busy for a while."

Zack and I sat alongside the river, watching the children at their best efforts trying to master the fishing rod so that they may catch something. I turned to look at Zack, while Bram tries to reel in a fish. It keeps jumping off his hook.

"Oh man, I thought I had him." Bram said a little frustrated. Seth laughed while Bram struggled with his catch. Zack turned to Bram and said, "Next one you will get my boy, don't you worry." Bram throws his fishing line in and sat watching the water.

"What troubles you my love?" Zack asked as I continued staring.

"Nothing my dear, just looking at my beautiful family. Whom I love, and it is such a pleasure to be here, enjoying nature, where we belong." I said.

"Yes, my dear, I find it so peaceful. It is a pleasure spending time with you and the boys. I am excited for the weekend, to celebrate your birthday."

"Zack, give me your hand." I took his hand and put it on my belly.

"Oh my, the baby is wide awake. I can feel her kicking."

"Just look Zack, I will ask the baby to show her hands. See what happens." I ask my unborn child to show her hands through my mind, and the baby pressed both hands against my tummy.

"What is that?" Zack asked astonished. "I can see both hands, that's fasinating! But how did you do that?" I looked at Zack and said,

"I can speak to her through my mind and she responds."

"What?" He said utterly bewildered. "Who is she and what are you talking about? We don't know if it's a girl or boy. I think we need to go back. You must be tired or confused, you need rest my love."

"No Zack, please calm down. I need you to understand that we are going to have a very special child with some sort of ability."

"What are you talking about? You definitely need rest."

"No, just feel."

"No! You are scaring me with whatever it is that you're saying, and with the baby."

"Zack please open your mind and try to understand what I'm saying and about to say to you. It is about our unborn child and me."

"Daina you scaring me now, please let's just go back to the house. You need rest."

"Zack please, I cannot do this without you. Believe me! I too was afraid and confused when I found out that I am not from here."

"What are you saying? Daina, you are not making any sense. Let's go!" Zack got up and called the boys to pack up so that we can leave and go back to the house.

"Boys come now, let's go! Your mother needs urgent rest." The boys looked confused at their fathers behaviour, but obeyed him and packed up to return to the house.

"Oh Zack, why are you overreacting? You spoiling their fun. We can still talk about things later."

"No Daina, we're leaving now and that's it. No more talk about abilities or special babies." I turned to look at Zack and said, "Okay. Let's go home." On our way back to the house, the boys couldn't understand why the sudden change of heart.

"Ma, what is wrong with Papa? He looks very upset. Did we do anything wrong?" Bram asked quietly.

"No my son, your father is just tired and he needs rest. You and your brother didn't do anything wrong, so don't worry yourself. When we get home, you and your brother can find Langos and have a bit of play time with him."

"Oh yes, thank you Ma." He said and walked towards Seth to give him the good news. The closer we got to the house, the sooner the boys started running back. Excited to meet up with Langos. They called out to him and to their dismay, Langos was nowhere to be found.

"Good afternoon Nana, Uncle Pat and Aunt Olia. Where is Langos? Ma said we could play with him."

"Hello boys." Everyone greeted back.

"Langos is resting after his morning walk. He will play with you later, but first go wash up and prepare for lunch. Where are your parents?" Asked Pat.

"They are almost here. We decided to run ahead. Papa is not in a good mood Uncle Pat."

"Don't worry my boys, your father must be tired. Off you go." And the boys ran into the house towards their bedroom. Nana turned to look at Pat and Olia and said,

"I hope Daina took the time to start explaining the story to Zack. And here they are. We shall see how things went."

"Good afternoon everyone." I said. Zack nodded his head and made his way to the bedroom.

"Zack what's wrong?" Pat asked, but Zack ignored him and carried on walking. Nana looked at me and said,

"My child what happened?"

"Oh Nana, I tried to explain to Zack about our child's abilities and about me. But he won't accept it or at least hear me out." I burst into tears. "I am so tired and worried Nana. I know he does not believe me. What can I do?"

"Before the night has come, Zack will understand and believe everything. Trust me." Nana said as she led me to the kitchen.

"My child, you need to relax. We will be here, unless you want Pat to help you to bed?"

"No Nana, I am okay and comfortable. I think Zack may need his space to think about what I've told him." I took a few deep breaths in to calm my unsettled heart. I could hear Nana and Olia talking quietly in the background of my conscious as I drifted away into a strange yet peaceful sleep. Given that I fell asleep while sitting on a chair in the kitchen of course. Olia decided to join Pat on the porch while Nana prepared lunch.

As I rested in the kitchen, Zack was upstairs thinking about everything I had told him in disbelief. He could not stop thinking about the unborn child and that we were going to have a baby girl. "But how does she know?" he questioned himself, "And the hand prints appearing? And so clearly. What is going on?" he thought, trying to calm himself down. He felt awful for changing the plans, cutting the fun day short.

"Oh how stupid of me," he said talking to himself, "I upset the love of my life and my boys. How can I make this up to them? They might not forgive me?" Zack felt emotional as he thought about how to the day played out. And then he heard a soft quiet voice answering back while he questioned himself out loud. "Papa no-one is upset with you. We love you." He jumped up and said, "Who is there? What do you want?" Feeling very frightened, "Don't be scared Papa, we will meet very soon. Open your mind to Ma's words." Zack now sitting straight up on the bed, cannot believe what he has just heard. And what he is feeling. The fear he once had a moment ago changed to comfort like no other, coupled with love. He thought of me immediately. He thought about how I would react if he told me what just happened to him. He slowly got off the bed, checked on the boys and saw them playing a board game.

"Boys, I will call you when lunch is ready."

"Okay papa," the boys responded. Zack made his way to the kitchen and as he entered, he saw me sleeping in Pat's comfortable chair. Nana is standing next to the stove.

"Are you feeling a little better now, after your rest my child?" He hesitated at first, because he thinks he might sound crazy or foolish. "I'm okay Nana."

"You don't look okay my son. It looks like you've seen a ghost. What troubles you? You know you can always speak to your Nana." She reassured him.

"I am okay, just a little hungry I think." He said and smiled. Nana walked towards the kitchen door that led to the porch and said,

"Okay my son. You relax, lunch will be ready in 30 minutes." Nana joins Pat and Olia on the porch.

CHAPTER 4

HEARING IS BELIEVING

Zack made himself comfortable in the kitchen, and I eventually woke up and saw him staring at me.

"You okay my dear?" I asked as I yawned, "sorry I don't know what came over me. I had this sudden burst of exhaustion and fell asleep right on this chair. I have to say, it is incredibly comfortable. You should try it sometime."

"Okay my love, yes I am fine and I am sorry about earlier this morning. It was an awful thing to behave the way I did. I hope you and the boys are not upset with me."

"No my love, why would we be upset? Tomorrow brings another day for you and the boys to go out fishing or bird watching. Whatever you boys decide to do."

"I think, I will stay home and relax a bit and give you boys some time to bond." I said.

"No my dear, we always love having you around and you are far better than I. You're good at listening and understanding the boys' complaints or demands." Both Zack and I started to laugh. Nana walked in from the back porch and said, "Who is tickling who? You make me want to join in on the fun."

"Oh Nana, we're laughing at the fact that the boys complained a lot today because they hadn't caught any fish. Even though, sometimes they would forget to put the bait on their hooks. I saw that with my own eyes, but decided not to say anything and let them figure it out for themselves."

"Well boys will be boys." Nana said,

"Are you both ready for lunch? It will be ready soon."

"Yes Nana. Would you like me to call Pat and Olia?" I asked.

"That's alright, they already know." As Pat and Olia sat on the porch, they could feel a light gush of wind flowing through the air.

"His here." Olia said. Pat got up to call Nana. She was on her way already, knowing the Tree spirit King had arrived.

"Daina? Are you coming? We have a visitor"

"Nana…" I rolled my eyes towards Zack, "What about the boys?" I asked out loud.

"No need to be concern my child," Pat said, walking in after he heard all my questions. He made his way to the staircase, lifted his hands towards his mouth and mumbled his famous words that would stop time. Pat returned to the kitchen, I looked at Zack watching Pat.

"Okay Pat, what was that? What were you doing? And who were you talking too?" Zack asked.

"My son, relax. All will be revealed soon." Zack jumped out of his chair and looked around the kitchen.

"What is going on?! You guys are creeping me out!"

"Zack, please calm down. Have a seat. You're upsetting the baby." I said to him.

"Baby? Baby you say. Daina! I had the strangest experience today. I heard our unborn child speaking to me. How is that even possible? I think I'm losing my mind."

"No my love, have a seat please." I turned to Nana.

"Nana do something please." Nana slowly took Zack by the shoulder and calmly said,

"Please my son, sit. I will pour you a nice cup of my special tea. It will calm you." And Zack slowly sat down, putting his hands on his head not knowing what to say or think. Nana poured Zack a cup of tea and gave it him.

"My child, I think you should stay and sit with Zack, we will see to our visitor." She said to me and I agreed. Pat and Nana made their way out of the kitchen door onto the porch, where the Tree Spirit King awaits them with Princess Olia.

"Greetings Mother. You called upon me?"

"Yes my friend, there is an important matter to discuss. Tree Spirit, have you ever heard of an object called The Kahul of Darkness?" Nana asked.

"Yes Mother, but the object was lost centuries ago and no creature dares speak of it. Why ask about the object? It is a very dangerous object to wield."

"I am aware of the danger. It has been brought to my attention recently that Ciandra is searching for the object. To be able to control the Bingjie and stop the birth of the Child of Light. And the Queens return to Famos. My dear friend, will you be able to find the exact location where the object might be hidden?"

"Mother, I will search far and wide, and call upon my Spirit dwellers to help seek out the hidden object."

"We don't have much time my friend. We will seek help from Lady Salira as well, as soon as we reach the lake in one day's time." Nana said.

"I will leave you now Mother, to start my journey." Said the Tree Spirit King, and glides with the wind down the path and disappears into the woods.

Zack and I were patiently waiting in the kitchen for their visit to be over. Zack turned to check the time and saw that the clock has stopped.

"Daina, I wonder what's keeping the boys? I need to check for batteries, because the clock has stopped." He pointed out innocently.

"It's not the clock that has stopped my love, it is time itself, that has stopped." I said with a smile on my face. Zack looked baffled as I explained to him.

"Don't be silly. How can time stop? That's impossible my dear."

"No. Why don't you go outside and see for yourself?" Zack and I made our way to the back porch and with an astonished look, he turned and said, "What is going on?" he noticed the water from the sprinklers had stopped midair. Each droplet frozen in time. Pat saw Zack walking towards the steps with me following right behind him.

"Are you okay my dear?" he asked.

"Daina?!" Zack said, turning back suddenly and asked,

"What is this?" I turned towards Pat, put my hand out and said, "My dear Zack, I would like you to meet Father Time. And Nana is Mother Nature. Princess Olia is my first cousin once removed." Zack looked at everyone. He could not believe what he was just told.

"Who? What? Daina, what's going on?" He asked. Nana got up and slowly walked towards Zack, "My son, come. Let's go inside. We can speak there." Nana took Zack by his arm and followed after everyone else.

"Now have a seat, in Pat's wonderful chair. You definitely need it now.Zack are you ready for me to explain everything to you?" I asked as he sat down.

"Okay. I am a bit confused, so I will try to get what you are about to say." I began explaining to Zack my birth place, my parents and our unborn child. He carefully listened to try and comprehend what I was saying. But to my dismay, I do think Zack is still in disbelief. However, I still need to explain the Bingjie to him and hope that he understands. Langos came walking through the backdoor, just as I was about to tell him.

"Okay Daina, this really is a lot to digest. And I am not entirely sure if what you're saying is true. There is an explanation for everything." He said. At this moment, Langos turned to look at Zack and said, "Zack." Immediately Zack jumped out of the chair frightened and said, "YOU CAN TALK?! I knew there was something peculiar about you. But you can talk. You're a dog, that's not possible."

"No, I am merely in a form that you humans would accept. I am the Shield." Langos said.

"I cannot believe I am talking to a dog. The boys will be over the moon and freaked out at the same time."

"No Zack, the boys cannot know. If they find out, their lives will be in grave danger. You cannot tell them anything please." Zack looked at Langos and said, "A talking dog. I cannot believe it. So, you understood everything I told you back at home. Even though you were so stubborn."

"No Zack. The Queen, the boys and you were in danger, that is why I did not want anyone to go outside. I could not expose myself to you or any human in the Plain of Mankind, it is forbidden."

"Okay Langos." He said. "Why me?"

"Well Zack, you are the gifted one that can wield any item created by the Creators. But first, we need to find the Kahul of Darkness before Ciandra does." I responded.

"The what of Darkness? And what items is Langos talking about? Daina this is crazy!"

"No Zack, pull yourself together! Open your mind. There is one last thing Zack."

"What now? I honestly think I have had enough."

"Really Zack? How do you expect me to feel? I just discovered who I truly am, literally a day ago. My parents are still alive and we can save them. And my baby girl will become Queen. Yes, I know it's a lot to take in, but I have accepted my destiny and I will follow the path. All the way, for the sake of my family and my people."

"What people are you talking about Daina?" Zack asked, still filled with doubt.

"The people of the Kingdom of Athela." I said while rubbing my tummy.

"Is the baby ok my dear? I hope this whole situation is not stressing her out."

"No, she's actually very calm at this moment. Would you like to speak to her?" I asked. Zack slowly made his way towards me. Put his hand on my tummy and felt how our baby move.

"Oh Daina, it's such a wonderful warm feeling. It's as though she knows that I am here." Nana stood and looked at both of us.

"Yes my son, she knows you are close. That is why she is eager for you to accept what Daina has told you. You will need to build your bond with her, to face the road ahead." Zack had a look of amusement. "I will do anything to protect my family. Whatever lies in my path, I have to face it, and I will defeat it." He declared.

"Hold on my son, you first need to understand what you're going up against. It won't be easy, and it will be exceptionally dangerous and full of darkness." Pat said as he interrupted.

"Pat, I fear no darkness nor danger. I have courage and goodness in my heart to face anything for my family." We all sat and listened to Zack as he boldly declared his courage and will to fight, as though he had already accepted his destiny.

"What lies in the road ahead Nana?" Zack asked eagerly.

"Well my child. First things first. We have to travel to Lady Salira. She is the Lady of the lake and Protector of the Sea. We will need to request safe passage to be able to find the path that leads to the Domain of the Bingjie."

"What is this Bingjie?" Zack asked.

"It is a creature that possess great power, I myself have never seen before. The Lady of the lake will be able to tell us more about the Bingjie and its world. All I know, is that it lays beyond the waters of the Moeks, and no living creature dares to enter its Domain."

"Nana, why must we go through the Bingjie's Domain?" Zack asked.

"My son, the gateway to Famos is blocked by the young Trimos clan. They want to over throw the Kingdom and

Ciandra wants to claim the crown. There are different Cities we call Domain's in Athela. The Domain of Famos where Daina was born as Princess Liara, and the true Heir to the Throne. The Domain of Trimos where Ciandra comes from, and the Domain of Onasia is where we will travel, to meet Lady Salira of the Moeks, and that is the Kingdom of Athela. There is one more Plain that the Creators made, the Plain of Mankind, civilization. Combined all the Plains together, it's called the Realm of Ekna, which is also known as Earth." Nana said before continuing. "The Trimos clan cannot enter the domain I live in, while the Shield is up. I had to remove Princess Liara from Famos, minutes after she was born. The Creators would have banished her as they have banished both her parents to the Outer Realm."

"Outer Realm? What is that?" Zack asked.

"My son it is a place that Creators made that is filled with creature's and Beings from all the Plains combined. A dark world that for only one month of the year there is light and the rest is filled with darkness. There are horrible creatures who live there that will fill you with fear. I do not wish to speak more of this place because it leaves me sorrow filled to think about what Daina's parents have to endure. It was Daina's mother, Queen Liaana's last wish that one day baby Liara may return and claim her rightful place as Queen of the Kingdom of Athela. I had to protect her by suppressing her memory and power to be able to grow up as a normal child, hidden from the Creators. That is why we named her Daina. There is only one other pathway, and it lies beyond the Domain of Onasia. We will have to travel and find the doorway that leads to the Bingjie's Domain. It is a dark place, darkness controls everything. Once you have fulfilled and completed your task Zack, Langos will see the pathway that leads to the hidden palace steps of Famos. Daina carries the Child of Light and the child cannot be born in the Plain of Mankind, she has to be born in the Famos."

"Why Nana?" Zack asked.

"My children listen carefully. The unborn child is not like any other. She will not be born in the same way as all other human babies are born."

"What do you mean Nana?" I asked.

"Your baby will be born in a ball of light, that your body will create to protect her. You will become the beacon that will project the light. She will sense the stars alignment, and you will see a miracle happen before your eyes. And she will be born not only in flesh but also of light, in the Kingdom of Athela, as the Child of Light. Daina and Zack, you will see your baby girl grow from the light into the Being that she is meant to be. I hope both of you understand how important you are to all of us."

"Well Nana, I felt your answer. She just kicked me." I said after the little one had her say. Olia looked at Nana and said, "Mother, you must rest now. Let me prepare the table. Pat would you please bring everything back to normal, so that we may sit and have lunch?"

"Oh yes my child, that is a very good idea." Nana said. Zack got up and made his way to the staircase. Pat mumbles his words and Zack could hear the boys chatting away.

"Why was I not affected by time?" Zack asked Pat

"Well my son, once the baby spoke to you, she woke your inner being. I knew you would not be affected. Unless I put you in a time sleep, but that was not necessary." Zack stepped back and said,

"Inner being? Time sleep? That's okay. Nothing can surprise me anymore." Zack said before calling the boys to get done. The boys came rushing down the stairs, straight into the kitchen.

"Hungry boys?" Olia asked.

"Oh yes please." They both replied. Olia started dishing up the lunch and everyone sat quietly as they ate. After lunch was finished the boys asked to be excused to go back to their boardgame and off they went. Zack started clearing the table when Nana asked everyone to join her on the porch. Everyone started slowly making their way to the porch, while Zack was still cleaning the table.

"Daina, how do you feel now that Zack knows everything?"

"Well Nana, I am still a little nervous about the road that lies ahead, including this Bingjie creature. What will we do with the boys when we have to go see Lady Salira?" I asked.

"No need to be concerned." Olia interjected. "I will stay here and protect the boys. No harm will come to them."

"I will put them in a dream sleep, they will not be harmed." Pat added.

"My Queen no harm will come to them. I will shield them during their dream sleep." Langos reassured me.

"What kind of Being are you Langos? You mentioned that you are the Shield that protects everyone. Truly amazes me." I asked.

"Well my Queen, the time will come when all will be revealed. And the path we all have to take will allow me to show you who I truly am. But for now, this is my form." Nana slowly sat down on the porch chair, listening to what Langos was telling me.

"Daina, you will understand everything Langos has told you once you enter the Kingdom of Athela." Nana said. Zack made his way to the porch and sat down next to me.

"My love, are you okay?" I asked Zack.

"I think I'm okay. Given the circumstances. But as I mentioned earlier, I will protect my family no matter what. How do you feel knowing that you have a whole Kingdom?" He asked.

"The Heir to my throne is right here." I took Zacks hand and placed it on my tummy. "She will become the Queen, and we will support her during her reign."

"Nana, what about the boys? Will they ever see their sister?" I couldn't help but feel concerned.

"No need to be concerned. Once you and Zack have fulfilled the path you have to walk, everything will take its place. They will never lose their sister. If the prophecy is fulfilled."

"Okay Nana, I understand. We will do what needs to be done."

"When will we know when to start our journey to Lady Salira?" I asked after a brief moment of silence.

"When the fourth star aligns with the Outer Realm, and the birds sing no more. You will hear the sound of calling, for that is the time." Nana replied

"I don't understand."

"Oh Nana," Pat interjected before he turned to look at me.

"In the next few days, we will need to start with our journey."

"My apologies child, I was counting the days according to the Athelian time. But yes, Pat is right, we have one day."

"Okay, so that gives us time to let everything sink in and prepare for the days ahead." I suggested.

"Mother, I need to rest. I feel I have become weaker. Time is different in the Plain of Man and I will need my strength if I might be called upon." Olia said.

"Yes child, I do understand. You may go and rest to restore your strength." Nana said.

"Thank you. I excuse myself and will see everyone very soon." Olia left and called it a night. Zack and I thought it a bit strange, "What does she mean?" I asked Nana.

"Olia is a very special person, and as one who is gifted, you need a lot of rest. Daina, you and Zack will see what I mean once you are in the Kingdom of Athela. We all will need a lot of rest before we go on our journey." Nana said. Pat notices how intensely Langos is watching me. "Is everything okay Langos?" Pat asked, "Yes Father," Langos replied, "I am restoring my strength. Healing Dajeti has taken a lot out of me." I placed my head on Zack's shoulder feeling rather tired.

"Oh my love, why don't you go rest."

"I'm okay for now, thank you." We got up and headed for the room. On our way to the room, Zack picked up a very bad smell.

"What is that?" He asked, "It reminds me of something?"

"Oh yes, that stinky wood." I said, "Remember the one you found years ago, someone must have burnt it or got it wet."

"I wonder if the boys brought it with."

"Brought what?" I asked.

"The wooden horse, remember?"

"I told you to get rid of that horse after you got splinters in your hand."

"I forgot Daina. I left it in the lounge."

"Please Zack, would you go and check, the smell is really getting to me." Zack made his way to the boy's bedroom where he found the boys playing their boardgame, but no wooden horse insight.

"Boys, can you smell something strange?" Both boys turned towards Zack and said,

"No Papa, we can't smell anything."

"Did either of you bring that wooden horse that was at home?"

"No Papa."

"Okay, you enjoy your game and no noise okay? Your mother is going to rest." He said rather confused yet certain of what he smells. Standing in the hallway, the strange smell grew stronger, but he could not make out where it was coming from.

"Zack, did you ask them why they brought that horse?"

"Oh no, my dear, the boys never brought it with. It must be someone else burning that same type of wood or something. Please try to not let it bother you."

"Okay I will try. I'm going to read for a bit, will you call me when it is close to supper time?"

"Sure." Zack still looking puzzled about the smell, sat on the chair in our bedroom. Wondering where it could be coming from. He made his way back to the porch where Nana and Pat were sitting.

"Nana, can you smell something awful? Daina and I have been smelling it since we got to the bedroom."

"What smell child? I can't smell anything." She answered. Langos smelt what Zack was referring to the closer he got to him.

"Mother, that smell is from the Forbidden Tree."

"No Langos, it can't be! That Tree only grows in the Outer Realm. How can the both of you smell it?"

"I can smell it, Mother. It is surrounding Zack." Langos said.

"But I do not understand why. Zack, I have sensed that smell before at your house. But could not place it because my senses are different when I'm on the Plain of Man. The Queen spoke of a wooden horse carving, I could sense something was not right when you touched that wooden horse at your house." Langos said.

"Langos you are right. I warned the boys not to ever get it wet, because it gave off a very bad smell. However, the boys said they left it at home. How can this be that you smell it on me?" Zack asked

"Where did you find this wooden horse?" Nana asked Zack.

"Well Nana, I found a piece of wood laying in the woods many years ago and when Bram was younger, I carved a wooden horse from it for him.

"Zack, where did you find this piece of wood?" she asked again

"I found it in the Forbidden Woods. Daina and I were younger, and I kept it all these years."

"Oh my child, how could you?! I forbad both of you from ever going into that part of the woods. It is a dangerous place for children."

"Sorry Nana. Daina never entered, she was too scared. I went alone. I fell into a deep hole and found a piece of wood, that was it. We both were okay, so no need to worry."

"No Zack, there is a certain time of the year, when the Forbidden Tree grows in all the Realms at the same time. It is a very dangerous tree."

"Mother, I need to speak to Dajeti. He might know more about what we are dealing with. I have no memory or knowledge of this tree." Nana agreed and Langos ran towards the woods to see Dajeti.

"My child, what did Daina say about the smell?"

"She just thinks it's a bad smell. We both know that the only time it smells is when it gets wet. I don't understand where this smell is coming from now."

"Please Zack, go keep an eye on Daina. We will call you once Langos returns." Pat instructed Zack and he left. Feeling very guilty because of this bad smell, he thought to himself, 'maybe I touched that horse while we were at home and the smell is only revealing itself now. I should take a shower.' He walked quietly past the bed to the bathroom to take a shower. In the shower, Zack had flashbacks of the day he found that piece of wood. It was as though he was drawn to it. That's when he slipped and fell into a deep hole. He kept on shouting and screaming to get my attention. But it was as though no-one could hear his cry. He felt terrified. And that's when he found the piece of wood. And all of a sudden, he found himself out of the hole. 'How did I get out of that hole?' he wondered. As he made his way back through the woods towards me, he sensed something, but could not get rid of the wood. It was as though it was possessed by something. When he carved that beautiful horse he thought, 'what happened?'

"Oh no, I can't tell Daina any of this. She will be very upset with me. We already have such a treacherous road ahead of us and now this too? I think after my shower, I definitely need to rest." Zack told himself quietly while finishing up in the bathroom.

CHAPTER 5

THE WALKWAY TO THE HIDDEN

While everyone is resting in preparation for the road ahead. In the Kingdom of Athela, on the Domain of Famos, Prince Thelon is visited by the Great Seer. Thelon is sitting at the throne room table, reading through books of the past from the Kingdom and making notes for the preparation. The books are filled with thousands of pages, where to begin he thought. Princess Olia and her visions came to mind, when he sensed that the path ahead for the people of Famos, might be more dangerous than expected. If Ciandra finds the Kahul of Darkness then all hope is lost. Nevertheless, he will fight for the people and for his Queen when the time comes. He came across a chapter in the book of the Forgotten Touch, where he discovered something that is more of a riddle then a question.

"What is this?" He said out loud to himself and the doors to the throne room open.

"My Prince, it is I, the Great Seer Hiladra. I humbly request an audience with you. I can see something is troubling you my Prince, may I be of assistance?" Hilandra can sense his troubled mind, but he cannot see the trouble that haunts him. The Prince had a special gift; the ability to block all visions of his thoughts, not allowing anyone to see what troubles him.

"Great Seer! You may come forth, I am troubled with a question or riddle, if I may. Which I have discovered. However, I cannot see past the words that is written or understand the meaning of the phrases that is written."

"Oh my Prince, some words are not always easily understood. For there are hidden meanings within those phrases. What might these words be, if I may ask?"

"Here you may have a look. I am unable to make any sense of anything, my mind is troubled because I have not yet heard from my daughter."

"My Prince, do not fret. Your daughter is well. I can sense her calm demeanor; she has made her way to Mother and Father and has found the one that cannot be named." The Seer takes the book and glances over it and says,

"My Prince these words cannot be spoken out loud, nor can it be spoken in this room. We have to go to the Room of Wisdom, that is cloaked from all preying ears and eyes. My Prince, we need to go, for time does not wait." And off they went to the Room of Wisdom. Hilandra takes the book and coverers it with his robe. The Prince walked through the palace garden. It is filled with bright beautiful flowers and trees that bear leaves of colour. Famos is a place of brightness and beauty, and its people are peaceful Beings. They live in a city made of ripple glass filled with colour. There is magic that lies deep within its foundation and the surrounding woods. The Room of Wisdom was at the end of a long downward staircase and passage. There were writings on the walls, ceiling and floor of this passageway. Which led to one door.

"What are these writings Hilandra? I have never seen it before."

"My Prince, it is there to protect us from the unseen. All will be revealed soon. Please, allow me." Hilandra pointed to the door that led to the Room of Wisdom. On it was strange writing that Hilandra could read and understand. Hilandra spoke in a language that was not known to the Prince and the door opened.

"My Prince, you may enter." As the Prince enters through the door, he quickly realizes that this is no ordinary room. And it may be a different place entirely. He walked into a forest filled with mountains and lakes, in broad daylight. It is evident that this is not part of the Palace.

"What is this place Hilandra?"

"This place was created by the Fallen One, many life time's ago. Certain things that could not be spoken of or could be brought to light is kept in this hidden Realm."

"What are you saying Hilandra? A Realm within a Realm; how can that be?"

"My Prince, it is a place for keeping knowledge and for safety from the Creators."

"Why Hilandra?"

"Centuries ago, when the Creators created our Realm, there was but one Creator that wanted no part of any creation and drifted through the Universe. Like a window that carries sound. When the Realm of Ekna was created, it was drawn to this Realm. But as it entered the Realm, it was not able to keep its form and full power. Because it was not from this Realm, so part of it became adrift through the Universe."

"What happened to it Hilandra?"

"The Seers found the Being who created this Realm within a Realm. In order to protect itself and the knowledge of what was to come. It placed itself into a deep sleep, until the right time comes for it to reveal itself."

"Where is this Being?"

"I cannot reveal the Beings whereabouts. It is on a path that is unknown, for it does not have the ability to see it for itself, and I the Great Seer cannot speak of it. I have sworn an oath to the Seers of the Realm, to only reveal the truth to the true Heir of the Kingdom of Athela."

"Hilandra, who else knows of this Being?"

"I cannot say. For they will be in danger if word travels around the Kingdom."

"I will not speak of it."

"It is best that you do not know. The Being will reveal itself soon enough."

"The words in this book Hilandra, what do they mean? *Thou whom hath not risen in the times of thy choosing, the air shall be captured by thoughts of finding the lost. To stand as one, that thy may be complete. For sayeth the chosen one, will destroy or rebuild whatever she so desires.* What does this mean?"

"It means two that become as one, and the prophecy needs to be fulfilled. The Queen has to take her place. We need to send word to the Princess, the Shield and Zack. They will need to find the Forbidden Tree, for it will have the answers for them. I cannot see what the message will be for them, only they will know and understand. That is all I can say for now. My

Prince we need to go, please do not speak of this place to anyone, for it will not be safe and it will be made known to the Creators."

"I swear to you, as Protector of the Realm, Great Seer, I will not speak of this place." They left for the Palace throne room.

Once in the Throne room, Hilandra turns to the Prince and says;

"I will send word to Princess Olia on behalf of you."

"I would appreciate that Hilandra. Please ask my daughter to stay safe and fulfil the prophecy."

"I will leave you now my Prince." Hilandra left for the woods to get closer to Dajeti, knowing about the Trimos clan. When he reached Dajeti, he whispered his message into the air and allowed the wind to carry it safely. Princess Olia will be the only one who is drawn to the message.

CHAPTER 6

THE FORBIDDEN TREE

Zack and I rested, while Langos made his way to Dajeti. He noticed in the distance that Dajeti was awake, but by whom? He thought. As he got closer, he could see the Tree Spirit King standing before Dajeti.

"Langos? What has brought you here before me?" Asked Dajeti.

"Wood Keeper, Tree Spirit, I have a question to ask."

"You may proceed."

"Please tell me if you know of the Forbidden Tree, where in our Plain does it grow?"

"Why ask about a cloaked tree Langos?" Tree Spirit asked.

"Well my friend, we have come across a rather peculiar smell. Many years ago, Zack fell into a hole and found a piece of wood. He brought it back from the Forbidden Woods and it had a very peculiar smell."

"Yes Langos, that is the wood from the Forbidden Tree. How was Zack able to hold onto it or see it? No being can touch the Forbidden Tree, it is impossible." Dajeti responded

"No Dajeti, the Forbidden Tree only reveals itself to those it chooses. It is not a tree like us, but rather a Being from all the Realms that only appears once a year. For the rest of the year, it dwells in a Realm that is unknown." Tree Spirit answered. "Langos, there is a reason the Forbidden Tree revealed part of itself to Zack, you must ask him how he has stumbled across this piece of wood. There might be something of importance." While Langos discusses the Forbidden Tree with the elders, Nana and Pat sat awaiting his return, and Princess Olia joined them.

"My child, why are you not resting? You need all your strength." Nana asked. The Princess stood and gazed her eyes to the woods. She turned to look at both Nana and Pat and said,

"I was woken up by my Inner spirit. I need to make my way to Dajeti. I have been called by the Great Seer of Athela. My father has a message for me."

"You will not be able to return through the Wood Keeper, Dajeti has blocked the way." Nana reminded Princess Olia.

"No Mother, as long as I am close to Dajeti I will be able to receive the message from the Great Seer."

"Please be careful and do not be fooled by what you may hear or see. It might be a Trimos Seer trying to lure you to be able to see your thoughts and what you know of the Queen."

"I cannot be fooled by those who wish to harm the Queen. With my gift I can feel and sense the Great Seer and I can hear his words, as though my father himself has spoken. Mother, I will make my way to the Wood Keeper and will return soon." The Princess left for the woods.

Pat and Nana sat baffled by Princess Olia's news, but in high hopes that she may be right. Olia walked through the woods and saw Langos speaking to Dajeti and the Tree Spirit. As she approached them, all greeted the Princess.

"Princess, myself and the Tree Spirit have been awaiting your arrival. I cannot give you passage, but I am aware of the message only you will receive." Dajeti instructed. The Princess turned towards Langos and said,

"Langos I can see you have discovered the knowledge of the Forbidden Tree. I have been summoned to receive a message from my father, that is of great importance." The wind starts blowing with a soft breeze.

"My Princess, with the wind a tale was told. And it is only for you to hear." The Princess listened to the message that was carried by the wind and turns to Langos and says,

"Shield, we must return to the house. For there is a road that only you and Zack will be able to find." Langos turns to the Princess and says,

"What road?"

"Langos, there are many pathways we all need to take. Please go with the Princess, some things might become clearer to you with the new road ahead." Said the Tree Spirit. Langos and the Princess left for the house. They made their way through the woods back to the house where Nana and Pat eagerly await. Expecting some sort of explanation concerning the Forbidden Tree. As they made their way up the porch, Nana could sense the bewilderment from Langos.

"Langos, what troubles you and Olia? The message from your father?" Nana asked.

"Hold on my blossom, give them a minute or two to regroup." Insisted Pat

"Oh Pat, I am trying desperately to comprehend what may come but I'm afraid I'm at my wits end."

"My dear, there is no need to fret. We have all prepared for this and we will be able to take on anything. Please be calm." Pat reassured Nana.

"Mother, I assure you, do not fret. For my father sends his greetings and I have been informed of the Forbidden Tree. There is a road that leads to the Forbidden Woods. Langos and Zack are the only ones who may travel this road. They will need to seek out the Tree, and it will only disclose itself to them."

"Langos, you and Zack need to go on this day before the sun has set. Once you have found the Forbidden Tree, you may ask what you seek." Princess Olia gave instruction to Langos while Nana responds.

"My child, what do they seek from the Forbidden Tree?"

"Mother, my father and the Great Seer have discovered, from the book of Forgotten Touch, words spoken of great wisdom. Whomever the Tree reveals itself too can summon it. The Tree has chosen to show itself to the Queen, Zack and Langos. But only two must go and I have chosen Langos and Zack." Olia said.

While everyone caught up on the day's events outside on the porch, I was upstairs reading my book. Zack asleep next to me found himself in some sort of dream, but could not explain what he was experiencing. Everything he felt, including the cut he got from a tree branch, was surreal. The cut started to burn.

"But this cannot be real." He whispers to himself as he tried to figure out what is real and what isn't. "I'm dreaming." He convinces himself. But then he sees a bright light, guiding him to a beautiful place of colour. In the distance, he could see a dark mist covering a valley, that turned into a dark shadow. It appears to be getting closer to him, until it stopped right in front of him and spoke.

"Are you the bearer of hope? The one who thinks he can face me?" The shadow asked.

"Do you, little man? Do you really think you can defeat me?" Zack started shaking and sweating in his sleep.

"Before you enter my Domain, I will fill you with fear and darkness. I will destroy you!" And with that said, Zack woke up and could see a cut on his arm. He jumped out of bed at once.

"What is going on Zack? What happened to your arm?" I asked uncertain of what just happened.

"I don't know my love; I fell asleep and had a terrible dream. But it felt so real. I woke up with this cut on my arm." Langos rushed up the stairs; leaving everyone behind, entered the bedroom and saw Zack's cut.

"Zack, Daina, please come downstairs immediately." Langos demanded franticly. We rushed downstairs as he requested.

"Mother, the Bingjie made contact with Zack. Look at his arm." Nana took Zack's arm,

"My child, please give me your other hand. I want to see what you have seen." Zack did as he was told and Nana closed her eyes and saw what the Bingjie had spoken to Zack. I sat down, out of breath and asked,

"What is going on, please can someone tell me?" Olia turned towards me as Nana let go of Zack's hands and said,

"My Queen, one thing I know and can sense is that the Bingjie fears Zack. For it traveled so far in the hopes of persuading Zack to not enter its Domain."

"Zack, the dream you had was not a dream. It is a form of connection you have with the Bingjie, and like Olia said; it fears you. Do not mistake its fear for weakness, it is cunning and wise. You must not believe the words it had spoken to you." Nana advises Zack.

"You need to find the Forbidden Tree; I will summon the tree to disclose its whereabouts by communicating through an ancient tongue of the Seers. This language will call upon the Forbidden Tree to show you where is it hiding." Olia stretched out her hands in a suggestion to Zack.

"Give me your hands." Zack followed her instruction. Zack and Olia formed a bond using their abilities to find the Tree's hidden location.

"Repeat after me." She said to Zack

"*Trivolin Manutu Wesmin Pikasum Rectonda*" Zack did as he was told.

"What does that mean?" I asked.

"Forbidden Tree your hidden presence I seek. Show yourself. That is what it means when spoken in the tongue of man."

"My love, if this needs to be done; I will do what is necessary. Come what may, I will do anything to protect my family." Zack said as he turned to reassure me that everything will be okay. I'm pretty sure he can see that I am nervous about everything. Especially when none of us have any idea what is actually going on or what is about to happen. But if Zack is confident in himself, then I should be confident in him too.

"Come Olia, it's time to find this Tree." Zack said while offering his hands to Olia. She took Zack's hands and held it together and spoke the words; Zack immediately closed his eyes, fearful of what he might see if something is shown to him. *"Trivolin Manutu Wesmin Pikasum Rectonda"* she said, and Zack could feel an energy flowing through him. The Forbidden Tree spoke.

"Princess Olia what do you seek? The one that seeks me, stands before you. Oh, the fear within you, Zack is so tasty. Please give me more."

Olia responded. "Reveal your hidden place at once." Immediately Olia could see where the Forbidden Tree grew and she broke the bond between her and Zack by letting go of his hands. Zack caught her as she fell to the ground.

"What was that?" He asked her out of breath. "Who spoke to you Olia? I could not see anything, but I heard the voice." Nana ran towards Olia and placed her hand over Olia's head.

"We need to get them both inside." Pat insisted as he witnessed from the porch. Pat carried Olia inside as we made our way into the kitchen.

"Please Princess, you need to rest before you speak." I could hear the worry in Nana's voice.

"No Mother. Zack and Langos need to go on this day, before the sun has set and they may ask it what they seek. Zack, before you enter the woods place your hands on Langos and the pathway will be illuminated, and he will show you the way. But you must leave soon. The journey must be completed before the sun has set." She said almost breathless.

"What? Isn't that Tree dangerous and like the word says, Forbidden, why must they go?" I asked not too keen on this whole idea.

"Daina, my love. I will be ok, Langos will be with me. I have to go my love. I have made a promise to do anything, to keep my family safe."

"Okay, Langos please look after him and yourself. I cannot lose either of you." My eyes start watering as I tried to hold back my tears. Langos sat in front of me and within seconds the tears are gone and so are my fears.

"Better my Queen, you need not worry. We will be back before the sun has set." Langos said. Zack gave me a kiss on the forehead and they left for the path that leads into the woods.

When Zack and Langos reached the woods, he stopped to place both hands on Langos. Langos' eyes started glowing a dark blue colour and he turned to Zack and said,

"The path has been illuminated; we must hurry." Zack shuddered and stood back for a while.

"Please do not fear that which you see." Zack starts walking.

"Langos where will we find the Forbidden Tree in the woods?"

"Please do not mention why we are here. There are creatures in these woods that you do not want to wake."

"Creatures? What creatures? You are starting to freak me out Langos. Nana never told us about anything like that."

"Zack, please be calm. I can smell your fear. Breath, we have a long walk ahead of us."

"Okay dog, I will calm down."

"Please do not call me dog. I have told you before, I am merely in a form that humans accept."

"Okay Langos, but what are you exactly? Please do tell."

"Zack, all will be revealed soon. I cannot show myself in this Domain. if I do the Creators will sense my presence and all will be lost. Please Zack, you need to keep calm, I am not the only Being in these woods that can smell your fear."

"Okay Langos, sorry for all the questions. I am just a little nervous, and my arm hurts a little." Langos stopped.

"Zack, give me your hand."

"Why?"

"Would you like me to stop your pain or would you prefer complaining?" Zack gave his hand to Langos. He blew over his arm and white steam covered his entire hand. The wound started to disappear and he was healed.

"You are okay now Zack. Let's keep moving." Langos started walking again while Zack stood frozen in disbelief, before running after him.

"Thank you Langos." Langos nodded his head, and they carry on walking towards the Forbidden Woods. They came across a river. Zack turned to Langos and said,

"I don't remember this part. When I was a child, I remember it was not far from where the house was."

"That might be but now it lies deeper in the woods. Once we cross the river Zack, please do not speak. There are creatures that are awake during daylight and we need to be quiet. Once we have found the Forbidden Tree then we may speak."

"Langos what must I ask?"

"Zack, you will know what to ask when the time comes. Now no more talking." They approached the river and could see the Forbidden Woods on the opposite side. As they cross the shallow river Langos looks at Zack and says,

"Mind where you step in these woods, there are small creatures that will cling to your legs and will drag you into the earth. You do not want to cross paths with Crober creatures."

"What is a Crober?"

"No more questions, just observe where I step and walk behind me. I will lead the way." Langos whispered as they continued walking.

"Okay." Zack replied softly. As they made their way through the Forbidden Woods, Zack could feel a chill in the air. The woods are densely packed with dark-coloured trees, and no flowers in sight. Plants had powdery mildew on them and a screeching sound coming from the trees as the breeze flowed through the woods. Zack looked around not really paying attention of the dangers that surrounded him.

"Stop!" Langos said in a firm voice. Zack obeyed and turned, looking right at a solid slimy brown web. He could see a little creature moving towards him.

"Langos!" he shouted with a frighten voice, "I cannot move."

"Yes. I am aware. The Sektof confines their prey to one spot. It will then shrink you to whatever size it pleases and eat you." Langos walked towards the web and blew onto it and Zack was released. The creature vanished quickly with a screeching sound.

"What was that thing"

"Well, that was just one of the many beasts that live in these woods. There are worse out there, that will be happy to make a meal out of you. So, be more alert."

"Yes Langos, that was really an awful experience. I do not want to be eaten by anything else in this creepy place." As they moved further into the woods, they both heard a voice speak out.

"Do you seek the one that cannot be seen or have you come to join the Minchies? To be their dinner?"

"Langos, I am no one's dinner. Something already tried to eat me, please let's leave this place!"

"No Zack, keep calm. Remember what I told you about your fear?" And as Langos spoke, they could see movement through the trees.

"Langos what was that?" Zack whispered.

"Zack, remain calm. You need to focus on why we are here."

"Okay yes. So where is this Tree?" Langos stood still and not answering Zack. He knew the voice that spoke to them could be anything. The Forbidden Woods had all sorts of life forms with magical powers and might try to trick them into giving out information that could be passed on to the Bingjie.

"I call upon the voice that spoke." Langos said boldly.

"Show yourself!" The voice laughed and said,

"Who do you think you are? Walking through these woods and making demands. What do you want?"

"I will say no more. For the one we seek, is the one that knows he must show itself to us." Langos looked at Zack,

"I command you to reveal yourself to us, for I have a piece that belongs to you. That I know you would want returned. If you do not fulfil our commands, I will burn the part that's lost to you and you will never be whole again." Zack's demands were strong yet extremely baffling to him. In a few seconds, a light appeared in the distance and a big tree with red leaves stood high up and called to them.

"Please you may approach, no harm will come to you." Both Langos and Zack walked towards the tree.

"I know what brings you to me. I have smelt your bewilderment and fear since you entered these woods." Zack looked at Langos and said,

"What is this tree talking about?" And the tree brushed a branch under Zack's feet causing him to fall to the gorund.

"You call me a tree? I am a Being! I do have many forms but chose this form to blend in this Realm as part of these woods."

"That is not necessary Being, we do not know your name. What must we call you?" Langos said.

"Langos, you know my name very well." Zack slowly got up, dusted himself off and said,

"Why did you have to do that, stupid tree."

"Zack, I accept your ignorance. But just remember, the Bingjie beast that you will face, will not accept your arrogance. Remember its words spoken to you, you little man. It called you." The Being continued, "Yes you, you have a lot to learn. You are going to face an ancient creature that no-one has ever seen or dare speak of."

"But Being, how will I be able to defeat the Bingjie? We only want safe passage for the Queen to be able to give birth to our child."

"Zack, you already have that which you seek. Only you can reveal its place, but remember there will always be a price to pay for what you seek."

"Where can I find the Kahul of Darkness?" The Being laughed before responding,

"I thought you would never ask. Well you should know Zack; you were the one that found it. I hid the Kahul for centuries, but it found its way to you."

"Excuse me, what are you talking about?"

"Zack, have you never wondered how you got out of the hole you fell into so many years ago? It was I who lifted you out and guided you to carve the wooden horse. I also warned you not to get the wood wet, because it could reveal the Kahul to the Creators. The Kahul chose you to be its protector for all these years, and knew you were the Forgotten One that could wield its power. The Kahul is hidden within you Zack, it has shown itself to you when you were in the Plain of Mankind. Remember the burning sensation you felt when you touched the wooden horse on the floor? And when you held it under the running water? You saw the markings appear as though it was burnt into your flesh. The markings that were revealed to you belongs to the Kahul. It has become part of you and formed itself from your wrist, completing its mark over your entire right hand and forearm. Zack, you are the only one that may request for it to show itself. But remember these words I speak, within the Kahul there is darkness it seems. Langos, we will meet again very soon and then you may ask my name. But for now, you must leave this place, the Dark Ones and the Minchies will awaken and will sense Zack."

"Being, do you know what lies on the road ahead of us." Zack asked hoping to get a clear answer.

"Zack, you really are a special human. You will have to open your mind and balance the Kahul. For it can be used for Darkness, but also for Light. Choose well Zack; for you will be the only one that can create your own destiny. One wrong choice, can cause an entire destruction. Keep the Kahul hidden, and only call on it when needed. Remember, Ciandra from the Trimos clan has sent out creatures to look for it. There is one more thing. A command needs to be spoken for you to wield the Kahul against the Bingjie. But the only Being that knows these words of command is the Bingjie itself. It will not reveal the words to anyone, but there might be a way for you Zack. Only you will know when the time comes when you face this Being. That is all I can say for now." The Being slowly disappears as Langos and Zack quickly make their way out of the Forbidden Woods. Langos can sense they are being watched.

"Come now we must hurry. There are creatures that will wake just before the sun sets and we don't want to cross paths with them."

"Okay Langos, but I can only walk as fast as my feet will carry me. I am trying to keep up, but you are walking extremely fast." As Zack spoke, Langos stopped.

"Stand still, we are being followed. I am not sure by whom or by what, but stay close to me." Zack moved closer to Langos and stood still. The sun was slowly setting and through the dim light of the trees, Langos saw small figures moving towards them.

"Who is there? Show yourself?!" He heard a small voice.

"It is I, Thorpet from the Fixen clan. We do not mean you harm, we only wish to give you safe passage to Mother and Father." As they stood Zack saw small flower type creatures.

"What are they Langos?"

"They are from the Kingdom of Athela. Although I am not sure why they are here." He responded to Zack.

"Thorpet, what brings you to these woods? Why have you left the Kingdom?"

"Shield Langos, there are many of us that fled in fear when Queen Liaara was banished, because of the Creators. Mother gave us permission to live in her Domain and we have sworn to protect the Queens child." In the distance through the trees Zack saw more forms of life moving closer. They walked on three skinny legs and had two big heads, facing opposite directions. Long floppy ears, and its body was covered in purple and red stripes. It had a long bushy tale, and one of the heads yawned and Zack saw its sharp green teeth.

"Langos, look." Pointing his finger in the direction of the creature.

"What is that? Let's go before they eat us." Thorpet stood high on his twigs that were actually his legs and said,

"No they are peaceful Beings that feed on the earth. They eat the grass you are standing on. They mean you no harm Zack. It is the Crober creatures that you should fear, you need to make your way back to Mother. The sun is about to set and the woods are not safe for humans."

"Zack let's go; we need to return before sunset. Everyone is waiting." The Fixen disappeared into the woods, but still kept a close eye on them as they headed back to the house. Both Zack and Langos made it out of the woods safely.

"Zack, are you okay? I was so worried, I thought you were lost." I was so relieved to see them.

"No my love, everything went very well."

"Your arm, it's healed. How did that happen?"

"My dear, I have a lot to tell you. But for now, I am so exhausted and hungry. I will tell you everything soon." We left for the kitchen.

"Mother, we met Thorpet on our path back towards the house. Very surprising."

"Yes my son, I thought you might see the Fixen as well. Beautiful little creatures, sworn to protect the Queen and the unborn child."

"Mother, the Being we met in the Forbidden Woods, I have felt that energy before. But I do not know where. It is a strange Being, but I felt as though our paths have crossed before. I asked for its name, but he would not tell me. He spoke of the Kahul. Zack will tell you more. The Being spoke to him about the past and the future. Zack has the knowledge and understanding of what the Being has foretold. Mother, I will go rest for a while. You may call on me if I am needed." Langos walked towards the kitchen where Zack and I were sitting. Nana slowly got up and turned to Pat and said,

"Come my dear, let's start preparing an early supper. Olia my dear child, you go rest. When supper is ready, I will call you." Nana and Pat walked towards the kitchen. Olia made her way to her room. Nana started preparing supper.

"My son, don't you want to sleep for a bit?" Nana asked Zack.

"Oh no Nana, I think I had enough sleep for now, I don't think I want to have another nightmare, like I had before."

"My child, that is done. Don't worry everything will be okay. You just need to believe in yourself, that's all that matters."

"My dear, please tell me what happened? You don't need to tell me everything just yet." I asked concerned.

"Okay, one thing I do know, is that was a very rude tree. Oh sorry, I meant Being."

"Zack, I see you have learnt." Langos interrupted.

"What happened?" I asked again.

"Nothing my love, just had a little fall that was caused by the Being. But before that a Sektof creature almost ate me. If it were not for Langos I would have been dead."

"Oh thank you my boy." Forgetting he was not a real dog and smiled.

"Yes, those are malicious little two-legged creatures. Utterly grotesque, I am petrified just thinking about them. My blossom, why have you allowed those little beasts into our Domain?" Pat asked.

"My dear Pat, nature needs balance and I have allowed these creatures from Athela into our Domain to keep the balance. Just to mention a few; the Minchies, Sektof and Crober creatures." Nana responded.

"Oh yes. Still cannot shake the unsettled feeling when I think about them."

"Yes that is why you are Father Time and I am Mother Nature. The Creators must have known you would cause mischief that is why you control time and not nature." We all burst into laughter.

"My apologies Zack, please continue." Pat said.

"Yes, the Being then spoke of the Kahul and told me I had it with me all these years and called me the Forgotten One.

"What?" Pat said surprised.

"Yes, can you believe it? I had it all this time, it is in the wooden horse." Zack turned to Nana and asked,

"Nana, what did the Being mean when he called me the Forgotten One? I do not understand what it meant."

"My son, your destiny has been shown to you. That is why you were drawn to Daina. You have an Inner gift that no other human possesses. My son, have you ever had strange experiences before throughout the years?"

"Oh yes Nana, just before our trip I told Daina about the day I was at work when the new clearing path was made in the woods. I went to view the site, and I couldn't help the emotional hurt feeling I got. It was as though I could feel the pain of the trees and plants that were being cut down. I had to leave the site immediately and went home."

"My son, that was your Inner gift. That is why you were drawn to Daina as a child because she is from Nature and you were destined to be together." I looked at Zack and could see how surprised he looked because everything Nana said was true and he could feel it.

"Nana, I understand." He said in agreeance. I turned to Zack and said,

"That stinky horse you mentioned, it's at home. We asked the boys." I said.

"No, it is here somewhere. The Being told me that I could call on it to show itself."

"Zack, be careful to not just call it." Pat intervened.

"Yes you're right, we need to make a boundary to protect everyone from it." Nana said.

"Oh no Nana, it will not harm anyone." Zack insisted.

"No my child, objects of power you cannot always trust them to behave accordingly."

"Mother, the Kahul is no threat to us. It will obey Zack. We need not fear it. It can be wielded for Darkness and Light." Langos said.

"Nana, the Being mentioned that there is words of command I have to speak in order for me to wield the Kahul. Do you know what that might be?"

"I do not know. But Lady Salira might know what the Being was referring to. She is a wise ruler. Children, we will start our journey in the days to come but we do have a dangerous path ahead. Fear not for we will find all the answers that we seek, very soon. Come now, allow me to start setting the table." Zack and I left the kitchen. I checked on the boys, told them to wash up for supper and headed for the bedroom to do the same. Zack got into the shower to wash away his adventures for the day. I heard Zack singing and couldn't stop thinking of how quickly the day had passed and wondered what kind of a Being Langos is, he obviously has power. Zack and myself cannot explain but I should not question anything, I have seen the care he has for all of us and thought I really could use some bath time to relax before supper. The bathroom door opened and Zack walked towards me.

"Have a bath my love, you need to relax I will be here waiting for you." I nodded in agreeance and slowly made my way to the bathroom. As I took my bath, I couldn't help thinking about this place we are going to see. Nana told me that it's under water. How can this be? I thought. I cannot swim. I started rubbing my tummy and said, "My baby, soon I will be swimming just the way you are in my tummy. What do you say about that?" I received no reply and started to wonder, what's going on? I thought perhaps she's sleeping and suddenly a faint voice said. "No Mama, I am awake and can hear your thoughts. I need to keep my strength, for your journey ahead. I might be called." I responded, "What are you saying my child?" With no reply I decided to relax and remain calm. Zack got dressed and checked on the boys. They were packing their toys away.

"Papa, is supper ready? I'm really hungry." Bram asked as he entered the room. He looked around and said,

"Your room looks nice and clean. Both of you may go downstairs to Nana. She might give you a snack or two, before supper." And off the boys ran. I felt relaxed after my bath. I got dressed for supper and that's when Zack came back.

"My dear, you do look lovely. Although I can hear your stomach rumbling. I think our little one might be hungry too."

"Oh yes, I am a little hungry. Where are the boys?"

"They went downstairs to get a snack from Nana."

"Not surprised, they always trying to get something from Nana. But they might not have any luck, believe me." I said and we made our way down the stairs towards the kitchen. As we entered the kitchen, the boys nibbling on some food.

"Oh boys, did Nana give you a snack?"

"Yes Ma, it's tasty and delicious." Seth mumbled while he was eating.

"Seth, swallow before you speak my boy."

"But Nana, it tastes so good. Could I have some more, please."

"No, you will spoil your supper young man." And both of them finished their snack and sat quietly.

"So, Ma are you excited for your Birthday in two days? I am so excited, I made you something cool." Bram said

"Yes my boy. I do look forward to it. I know it will be a fun day." Olia joined us for supper. Langos watched silently without any sudden movements, to not alarm the boys, or draw suspicion. Once everyone was done eating, the boys asked to be excused from the table so that they may finish their board game before bedtime. I agreed to only one more hour of playtime. Once they left, I turned to Zack and said.

"My dear, I can see you have accepted everything and I am really proud of you. I know when the time comes you will be able to defeat the Bingjie, as Olia said. The creature must have a fear for you and now that you have the Kahul it will fear you more when the time comes."

"My love, what I have seen so far over the past few days, I do believe in myself much more. Today we have come across strange peaceful creatures in the woods and now I wonder what the Kingdom of Athela is like. I can imagine a peaceful place, not like where we come from."

"Yes Zack, but remember we still have to find the pathway that leads into the Palace." I turned to look at Nana.

"Nana where will I deliver the baby? When we return to the Palace, won't the Creators wake up and discover us?"

"No my child, all will be well once we start our journey. More will be revealed to you and Zack."

"My love, do not fear for what lies ahead. I will protect you and our unborn child. I think it's time for us to say goodnight, we do have a long journey ahead of us over the next few days."

"I agree." I said, and both of us wished everyone a good night's rest and we made our way to our bedroom.

"My son, are you ready for the days that lie ahead of us?" Nana turned to Langos and asked.

"Mother, I feel as though something is amiss. But I do not know what it is. I assure you that I am prepared for anything that is asked of me and I will use my Shield, to keep the boys hidden from what is to come." Nana turned to Olia and said,

"My child, you need to rest. I can feel the weakness within you and you will need your strength."

"Yes, Mother, I agree and I bid everyone a restful evening." Olia said and headed for her room. Pat sat quietly watching everyone slowly disappear to their rooms. Nana got up to clear the table.

"My dear, have you thought about you know who? The one who has to take their place?"

"Why do you speak of this now? The right time will come. It is not our place to say anything, you know it is forbidden."

"Mother, what are you and Father speaking of? I do not understand the meaning of your words?" Langos asked a little baffled.

"Oh my son, do not let an old fool's words bother you. It is merely something that we all will witness soon enough."

"Mother, witness what?"

"Well my son the miracle of light. That is all I will say for now, because it is getting late and we all have to get a good night's rest."

"Pat, are you done?" Nana asked Pat.

"Yes my blossom." He responded.

"Langos, we bid thee a goodnight." And off they went to their bedroom. As Langos laid in the kitchen, he could not help but wonder about the what Nana and Pat were speaking of. He felt there was something they were hiding. Soon after, he slowly started to fall asleep.

CHAPTER 7

THE SONG OF BATTLE

As I woke in the early hours of the morning the sun crept through the window. I got up while Zack was still asleep. The house seemed quiet and peaceful, I took my book and sat on the chair and started to read. Zack slowly woke up reaching for my side of the bed, but quickly sat up when he realized I was not there.

"Daina!" He shouted frantically as he looked around the room and saw me sitting on the chair close to the window.

"Good morning. No need to be alarmed." While rubbing my tummy, "this little one was up early and I felt as though something was coming. But as you know my dear, there is always something new happening in our lives."

"Yes I agree. But at least for now you should rest your mind my dear. Focus on our baby girl. I am so excited and the boys will be over the moon with joy."

"Yes my dear. Although we should not mention anything to them about having a baby girl."

"Yes, I agree. My dear I will start getting ready for the day and then we can see who is up and perhaps go for a little early walk?" We both started to get ready and made our way out of the bedroom. Checked on the boys and heard no sound coming from their room. Walked downstairs and entered the kitchen. Langos was standing at the kitchen door looking at something I could not see.

"Good morning." Both Zack and I greeted. He nodded his head and sat down.

"Interesting day yesterday was it not Langos?" Zack said.

"Yes. But there is still so much we both have to face. But as Mother has said, everything will be revealed soon." Langos responded. Nana and Pat made their way to the kitchen from the porch.

"Good Morning, you're up? Pat and I had an early morning stroll." Nana said. Olia made her way into the kitchen and could sense something was wrong as Langos looked through the kitchen doorway towards the woods.

"Mother, there is something dark in the wind." She moved quickly to where Langos was standing and onto the porch with Nana behind her.

"Princess what is it? What do you see?" Nana asked.

"Mother, I need to send word to my father and the Great Seer. The Trimos clan are preparing their attack on Famos. They are hidden under a cloak of darkness. However, I do not know how to send my message because Lady Ciandra will be able to sense me." Princess Olia could barely finish her sentence when tears started to pour down her face.

"Mother what do I do?" She asked. Nana put her hands on Olia's shoulders and said,

"Do not be dismayed my Princess everything will be okay."

"My son you are the only one that will be able to pass through Dajeti, you need to go and carry the message to Prince Thelon and Hilandra." Nana instructed Langos. Nana and Olia returned to the kitchen.

"Nana, we heard you talking about *darkness*? Are we in danger? Does it involve the Creators?" I asked.

"No, my child. It is the battle Olia has foreseen, but today it seems her visions will be fulfilled. Lady Ciandra will attack Famos without prior warning. Langos will need to take this imperative message to the Prince."

"Mother, I will go immediately." Langos said

"Be careful in the Woods of Emaksa, there are dangers lurking in those woods. Please protect yourself and return swiftly." Nana instructed and Langos left. Langos ran through the woods as fast as he could. He could sense the darkness rushing for Dajeti. A piecing pain overcame his entire body as he appeared in front of the Wood Keeper.

"Dajeti, I can sense the pain you are experiencing." He said concerned and out of breath.

"Langos, it is Lady Ciandra's Trimos warriors. They are trying to break the Shield of Ringmos from the Plain of Athela. You must find the Seer Hilandra."

"Yes, Princess Olia has a message that I will deliver to her father."

"Langos there is something that has been woken up. A creature, but I cannot see it or why I had this vision. The Seer

Hilandra might know of what I have seen. I am becoming weaker, Lady Ciandra's dark craft magic is weakening the Shield from within. I do not know how long I can keep the pathway closed and hidden."

"My friend, give me passage and I will heal you from inside." Dajeti opened his doorway that led to Athela. Langos stepped inside and with his magical gift, he started glowing. The glistering light was warm and subtle, possibly overwhelming to a normal being. This light started healing Dajeti from inside out. The glistering light started to fade.

"Now my old friend you are healed, and I have shielded you with the Ringmos invisible Cloak. The doorway between both Plain's will be hidden from all Beings."

"Thank you, my Shield." Langos shields himself with invisibility and enters Athela undetected. He travelled along the pathway to Famos and noticed the Trimos warriors cutting through the trees looking for the hidden pathway that leads to Nana's Domain. The pathway to the Famos Domain lies deep in the Woods of Emaksa. And only he can see this pathway. He can also see little crystals reflecting different colours that make up the pathway. He snuck past a Trimos warrior undetected. Each warrior had their own shape and size, their feet looked like patches of moss plants grouped together but fossilized into the shape of a leaf. This is used for protection against sound. Their hands were made of densely packed bushes. And branches that were as sharp and as strong as an eagle's claws capable of destroying anything. They had scorching red eyes that could pierce through any soul without trying. Despite their hideous stature, they are quite strong but thankfully not as fast as Langos. He continued his journey on this path and noticed the Trimos warriors became fewer and fewer. In the distance he saw another creature watching him, but continued walking. Until he came across something sitting on the side of the pathway. As he got closer, a little voice spoke.

"Greetings to you Being. I am Wuka. What brings you to our woods? If I may ask. I do not mean you any harm." Langos looked at this little strange creature with one eye, two legs, four arms and one half of his body covered in scales, the other half in fur. A really strange creature he thought.

"How is it that you can see me?" The creature bowed and said.

"I am from the Gigga clan. We have the gift of discernment, the ability to judge well. If you are of good standing, then you cannot be hidden from me."

"Wuka, why have I found you on this path?"

"We saw you coming through the Wood Keeper and know that you seek the Prince and Hilandra. Shield Langos, the path you are venturing on is hidden from all Beings because it is crawling with Trimos warriors. You will not find your way. We have also hidden the path that leads to Mother's Domain. It is not wise for you to go further than this, but I will show you another way to the gates of Famos, the Gigga clan use to enter. Lady Ciandra is planning to attack on the next sunrise. We Gigga's cannot leave the woods to inform Prince Thelon of what is to come. We have to combine our gift to keep the pathway's hidden, but you Shield Langos can inform Prince Thelon of Lady Ciandra's plan. She has used the dark craft to block all vision that can reveal her plans to the Prince."

"Wuka, show me the way. We must hurry." And off they went through the woods. As they walked along the river Langos could see the green valley below and mountains which appeared upside-down. He looked at the mountains strangely and Wuka turned to him and asked,

"Is everything alright Shield?"

"Yes. The mountains look different in this Plain, compared to the Plain of Mankind."

"Yes, but it only appears to be so from this distance. The closer you are; the better things will appear. I have been to Mother's Domain; I know of that which you speak. My Shield we should speak softer, the wind echoes spoken words through this part of the woods." Langos looked around.

"But there are no creatures in sight. What are you referring too?"

"Shield, this is the Singing Woods. Anything spoken out loud will be carried by the wind and that will not bode well for us if the Trimos warriors are made aware of our location." Langos immediately kept quiet, nodded his head in agreeance and continued walking. They reached a point in the path where beauty lies all around them. Trees of different colours, beautiful Beings playing around a waterfall and laughter in the air. In the distance was a massive wall made of crystal stone that stretched as far and wide as the eye could see. The closer they got to the wall, the more colourful the plants and trees were. And suddenly, the gate of Famos appeared. Wuka stopped and turned to face Langos.

"Shield this is as far as I can go. I am bound to the woods and cannot go further or I will break the chain that keeps the pathway hidden." Langos thanked Wuka for helping him reach Famos safely. Prince Thelon sat down at the throne room table, when Hilandra returned.

"My Prince, we have a familiar Being approaching from Mother and Father's Domain."

"Is it my daughter?"

"No my Prince. The Being will make his presence known to us soon." Langos approaches the beautiful gates of Famos that stood high above the ground and covered in gold. He walked straight through the closed gates undetected to all because of his invisibility. Except one, the High Seer Hilandra. He walked past the Famos guard who was standing in a still, upright position. The Palace was surrounded by guards who kept a watchful eye over the entire Domain. A voice spoke to Langos telepathically as he got closer to the palace. It is Hilandra's voice.

"Yes Seer, I am here to deliver a message." Langos made his way to the throne room where Prince Thelon and Hilandra were waiting. As he approaches the door opens. He removed his invisible shield.

"Greetings Prince Thelon and Hilandra."

"Greetings." Thelon said and Hilandra bows his head.

"What brings you to Famos?" Asked the Prince.

"Is it my daughter Olia?"

"Yes Prince Thelon. I have brought word from the Princess and Dajeti. I have also witnessed the Trimos warriors trying to find the pathway to Mother and Father's Domain, in search of the one that cannot be named. The Trimos warriors are planning an attack on the Domain of Famos and Mother's Domain. The warriors are hidden in the woods waiting for Lady Ciandra's command." Thelon got up from where he sat.

"Yes Langos I have summoned the Protectors to prepare for a battle that might come." And as he spoke a loud roaring noise echoed from a distance through Famos and to the Palace. Before the Prince could speak, the doors to the throne room open and a Famos warrior appeared.

"My Prince, there is a disturbance coming from the Woods of Emaksa. It's something no Being has heard before." Langos and Hilandra were the only ones who could see what was happening outside.

"My Prince the battle is about to start we need to get in position." Hilandra warns Thelon and he moved quickly towards the window of the Throne room where he could see the entire Kingdom and woods. He could see the Trimos warriors approaching with Lady Ciandra riding on a Plunatra creature. He turned with a horrid look and said to Hilandra and Langos.

"Ciandra is riding the forbidden Plunatra. What do you know of this creature Hilandra?" He asked.

"My Prince, the Plunatra creature cannot be tamed by any Being. For it is cunning and has its own ability that is unknown to us. It will use its ability only when it feels threatened. It would appear that Lady Ciandra might be using dark craft magic to tame the beast. It spits acid venom that will melt anything in its path and much more." The Prince and Hilandra heard the voice of Lady Ciandra as she spoke to them telepathically.

"I, lady Ciandra claim the Throne of Famos and will be Queen of Athela. I will go to battle with you and destroy you with my mighty beast and Trimos warriors. You have until the sun reaches its peak for you to hand over the Throne to me. Who is the one that is hidden? Show yourself!" It would appear she cannot see Langos. He did not respond.

"Show yourself Being!" She demanded and Langos remained silent.

"I will find out who you are. One way or the other. Prince Thelon if the gates of Famos is not open by the time I have given you; I will destroy all Beings that live in Famos." Thelon turned to face Langos, baffled he said,

"Why could Lady Ciandra not see you? I do not understand."

"My Prince we should not concern ourselves of that which we do not know. We need to focus on how to stop her. The Famos army cannot defeat the Plunatra creature and with Lady Ciandra as its master, I do not see how we are to be victorious." Hilandra said. Prince Thelon sat down at the table very apprehensive and thought, *'heavy is the head that wears the crown'*.

"My Prince, please you need to be strong for all the Beings of Famos and the Plain of Athela." Hilandra continued.

"Please summon the High guard." Hilandra immediately summoned the guard and the High Guard. The throne room doors open and the guard walks in and bows before him.

"My Prince." Thelon got up and walked back to the window. He looked down at his Kingdom and realized that no-one was aware of what is about to happen.

"High Guard, inform all Beings of Famos to seek shelter in the hidden caves below. They will be safe if the walls of Famos is breached. Blow the Horn of Athela, only once."

"My Prince, the horn has not been heard for more than a thousand years?" He said surprised at the Prince's request.

"Yes, but now is the time for all Athelians to know that Famos is going into battle."

"My Prince, what about the Creators? Will they not hear the battle cry?"

"No, the horn must only be blown once. If blown more than once, the Creators will awake. Summon all the guards to prepare for battle."

"I will do as you command my Prince." He turned around and left.

"There is but one who is able to defeat this creature. I have sensed that Lady Ciandra does not possess the full power of the dark craft."

"Langos?" Thelon asked.

"Mother, she is the strongest Yungna that may be able to defeat this beast."

"Langos we need to summon Mother at once! But how? This dark craft has filled the woods, it is not possible to find safe passage or give word to Mother."

"When the horn is blown, Mother will know and she will come." Langos said while looking out the window. "Her Domain falls in both Plain's." As Langos spoke the Horn of Athela echoed through the Palace and travelled through the Plain of Athela.

"I do hope that the wind will carry the Song of Battle through the Plain of Athela and Mother hears our call." The Prince plead.

CHAPTER 8

THE BATTLE OF THE DARK CRAFT

When Langos left to find safe passage to deliver the message to Prince Thelon and Hilandra in the Famos Domain, we eagerly awaited for his return. I sat next to Zack and wondered about the events that has occurred. With concern in my eyes, I couldn't stop staring at Nana while she stood at the stove.

"Yes my child I do know you still have a lot of questions. I can sense it, but all will be answered soon." Nana broke my train of thought. In a moment she rushed to the back door and I heard an unfamiliar sound. Olia and Pat were apprehensive.

"What is that sound?" Zack could not hear anything.

"What sound Daina?" He asked. Nana turned and looked at all of us with an apperception.

"The Horn of Athela has been blown. My child, it is the battle cry."

"Princess your vision is about to come to life but there is more to the sound." Nana told Olia as she tried to figure out if there is more.

"What battle?" I asked.

"My child, the Tree Spirit King and Olia spoke about this battle. Lady Ciandra is about to attack Famos." Nana closed her eyes and within an instant she says, "Pat get my cloak and staff. Please my children, be not afraid of what you are about to see." Pat brought Nana her cloak and staff and as she put on her cloak, she instructed Olia and Pat to keep everything as it should be. "I am needed in Famos." She said.

"Mother, the pathway to Famos is crawling with Trimos warriors how will you get there safely?"

"My Princess, there are other ways for me to journey. This will only be but a blink of an eye." Nana walked to the middle of the kitchen, stamps her staff on the floor three times and a cloud of white smoke appeared surrounding her. In a blink of an eye, she disappeared.

Langos, Hilandra and Prince Thelon stood in the throne room waiting. A cloud of smoke formed and within a second Mother appeared.

"Mother!" Thelon said as he bowed his head in greeting.

"Langos my son you need to return to my Domain you will not be part of this battle."

"But Mother I can be of help, if assistance is needed."

"No, my son. You need to protect the one that cannot be named."

"Mother, how should I return? The passage through the woods leads to the battle ground."

"My son, I will give you passage please step forward." And she put her hand on Langos' head. He turned into a ball of light, smoke surrounded him and he disappeared. Once Langos disappeared, Nana turns to Prince Thelon and says,

"We must meet Lady Ciandra outside of the gates of Famos. There we will meet her in battle, I do not want her dark craft flowing through the Palace walls." Thelon nodded and they made their way out of the throne room, towards the Palace gates where the guards of Famos await the Prince.

"Hilandra, you need to gather the other Seers of Famos to speak the tongue of Zolcrad over the Beings of Famos. The magic will protect the Beings from this dark craft that Lady Ciandra will use once the battle starts. It will manifest in the Beings if not covered by the magic tongue."

"Yes, Mother." He said and Hilandra left to find the Seers. Together they will journey to the hidden caves where all the Beings are gathered. As Nana and the Prince approach the guards, the High Guard announces his presence.

"Hail Prince Thelon!" They all turn in the same formation, with an upright position looking in Thelon's direction. Their armour is made of strong steel that originates deep within the mountains of Famos. It has a glistering coat that blinds their enemies, allowing them to strike first. Their mighty swords are made from the Steel Tree that grows in the Deep Woods of the Domain of Onasia. Prince Thelon stood high on the steps that lead to the throne room with Mother Nature by his side, and spoke in a loud commanding voice.

"Guards of Famos. Today we will face a dark enemy that dares to challenge our Kingdom and wants to change the way of life of all our fellow Beings. We do not bow down to any Being that is not from royal blood descend. The Protectors of Athela has put this law in place until our true heir returns. Today we will crush these Trimos warriors and their leader Lady Ciandra and send them back to where they came from. Do not fear the Plunatra beast. For we have Mother, the strongest Yungna to protect us from this dark beast." Prince Thelon's delivery was powerful and firm. There was no cheering or outcry from the Famos guards for they are profoundly serious Beings.

"To the gates!" And they all turned with an incredible formation and marched towards the gates. The sun was almost at its peak, and the gates opened. The High guard called out a command.

"Protection formation!" And some of the guards formed a barrier around the walls of Famos. As Thelon and Mother moved through the guards, they could see in the distance Lady Ciandra sitting high on top of the Plunatra.

"Do not let this beast's saliva touch your armour for it will melt you to the core and you will be no more." The guards stand patiently waiting Prince Thelon's command. And Thelon awaits Mother's command.

"Remain here. I will speak to this beast. If it does not heed natures command, I will lift my staff and the battle will commence." He nods his head and Mother walked towards Lady Ciandra facing her army. She could see the mark of the dark craft magic in Ciandra's dark yellow eyes. Her face was covered in writing. Her long-rooted hands were covered with hard tree scales. Her once beautiful shiny horns was covered in a white moult, her pure Trimos nature. Mother could see all was lost.

"Lady Ciandra and Trimos warriors from the Trimos Domain, you come here before the royal bloodline and the Guards of Famos to lay false claim to the Throne of the Kingdom of Athela. You bring forth a beast that is forbidden to be tamed by all Beings." Mother spoke with a voice of authority. "If you do not heed my warning and leave, you will be crushed." Ciandra stepped forward in disobedience with a loud menacing laugh.

"You Yungna, Mother of all Nature, you have no power over me or my beast. My Trimos warriors will destroy these feeble looking Beings you call guards. I will take this Domain and all Domain's that is part of Athela and then I will attack the Plain of Mankind and enslave the pathetic little humans you care so much about." Mother walked closer to her and Ciandra continued, "You Yungna take one more step and my Plunatra will melt you to your core." Ciandra commands the beast. "Burn this Yungna!" The beast opened its red beak, and a green slime made of liquid and fire started to form. It pulled its head back with a squealing loud noise, and spat little green glowing fire slime balls out of its beak towards Mother. Mother immediately lifted the Staff of Algara and pointed it straight towards Ciandra and the beast. A white light broke out and vanquished the green slime into thin air. Ciandra started speaking in the dark craft language but it was too late. Mother's magical staff created a magical dome of light that formed around the beast and Ciandra. And her dark craft was contained. Mother stepped into the light and Ciandra yelled out commands to the Trimos warriors to attack. They tried attacking Mother but they could not break the shield. Prince

Thelon lifted his hand and the battle started. The Famos guard fought bravely. Lady Ciandra commanded the Plunatra to move forward and attack Mother again. Mother started speaking to the beast and the dark craft that controlled the beast could not overpower Mother's words. Still pointing the Staff of Algara at the beast she said, "Beast! You are from Nature and I am the Keeper and Destroyer of Nature. I command you to break the dark craft that binds you to this Being. You have the ability to do what I command. And return to where you came from at once. But if you do not obey these words spoken unto you, I will destroy you and you will be no more." Ciandra tried everything she had to get the beast to obey her. But she could not defeat Mother's power. The Plunatra threw Ciandra of its back and started hissing and growling at her. With a loud awful shriek, it tried to slash her with its spikey tail. She rolled out of the way just in time. It started stomping the ground in vengeance for enslaving it. Ciandra was trapped in this confinement. She tried to find a way to break free but could not for Mother's power was too great. Some Trimos warriors witnessed Ciandra lose control over the beast and abandoned the battle. They fled into the woods to avoid being captured or destroyed by the Famos guards. The beast turned back towards Mother and bowed his head in submission. Mother removed the protective shield. Lady Ciandra saw an opening where Prince Thelon fought mightily against a Trimos warrior. She mumbled her dark craft tongue towards him. Mother was preoccupied with the creature when Ciandra went ahead towards Prince Thelon. And so, began the fight no-one anticipated. Prince Thelon swung his sword at Ciandra and missed her by an inch. And even though his armour protected him from almost anything, her rooted hand pierced straight through his armour. Prince Thelon fell to the ground in agony. Her dark craft magic poisoned him from within and the wound was too deep to handle, preventing him from being able to fight back. He fell to the ground in defeat. Lady Ciandra saw the High Guard running towards her and she retreated into the woods with some of her Trimos warriors. Prince Thelon succumbed to his wound. The High Guard ran to his side while Mother dealt with the creature. The beast submissively walked towards Mother. She took her staff and knocked it five times on the ground. The solid ground where the beast stood, turned into sand and a gush of wind came down from the sky onto the beast. The wind blew in a spiral towards the ground and the Plunatra disappeared. Mother rushed over to Prince Thelon with great concern. The High Guard removed his chest armour. Mother could see that the wound began festering, as the infection runs through him. She knew that she had no power in her to save him, for the wound was formed from dark magic.

"Mother?" He said as he coughed up black liquid, firmly holding onto her hand, "What of the creature? And Lady Ciandra?" She moved closer as he held her, for she knew he was fading away.

"My Prince, I have sent the creature back to where it belongs. It will no longer bother any Being." Mother said to Prince Thelon. Some of the Trimos warriors threw down their armour and surrendered and the battle was over. The High Guard, still on his knees, turned towards Prince Thelon and said, "My Prince, we have lost Lady Ciandra she has escaped into the woods. What should we do?"

"You will not be able to locate her. She has covered herself and some of Trimos warriors with the dark craft. She has moved to the Dark woods. I fear if you should venture through those woods there will be no return." Mother responded to the High Guard.

"High Guard, gather the remaining Trimos warriors and throw them into the dungeons. Their fate will be decided once the Protectors of the Trimos Domain has been returned back into their place." Orders the Prince while battling to breathe.

"Mother, please tell my daughter not to weep for I will be with her always. The one that cannot be named must take her place, and the prophecy must be fulfilled." He said faintly as his Inner light started to fade.

"Yes my Prince, all will be done." Mother reassures him.

"You rest now and find your peace."

"Yes Mother, it was a great honour to have you as the Protector of Athela. I will join my fellow Beings of past time in the great light and feast with the Queens and Kings." He slowly took his last breath and his inner light was no more. Mother was filled with grief but knew she had to be strong for what was lies ahead. She could see the High Guard was filled with sadness because of the Prince's death.

"Do not be overwhelmed with grief, for our Prince fought bravely. Use that sadness and turn it into retribution. Famos now needs your utmost bravery to protect its Beings for anything else that may come."

"Yes, Mother." He said, standing in an upright position.

"High Guard, the Prince must be taken to the Room of Age. The Seer's will prepare him for his fallen journey." In the distance she could see the Seer Hilandra rushing towards her where he saw Prince Thelon laying. He fell to his knees filled with sorrow and said, "My Prince," and he bowed over his lifeless body.

"Mother, what has been brought upon us on this treacherous day?"

"Hilandra, it was Lady Ciandra and her dark craft roots that caused the death of our beloved Prince. But do not weep, for this day will not be in vain. The Prince's last wish was for the prophecy to be fulfilled and we will do as he wished." Hilandra called to the other Seer's for the Prince's preparation for his journey.

"Yes Mother." He said.

"We still have much work to do. Now is the time for us to gather our strength." She said. The High Guards called a special formation and carried Prince Thelon to the Room of Age.

"Hilandra, I will see to the fallen guards and those of the Trimos. They all fought bravely for an unfair cause created by one that is filled with greed and darkness. They will become one with the land where their bravery will forever be remembered through the soil of the Plain of Athela." She lifted her staff and spoke. The ground trembled and the land turned to soil. The fallen sunk into the ground as their remains became one with the land, next to all the other fallen Athelians.

"Mother, I hope this is the last we will see of Lady Ciandra and her Trimos warriors." Hilandra said.

"When I spoke to the dark craft that has a hold over Lady Ciandra; I heard the words to seek the Deep Darkness. I do not understand what that meant."

"I have seen those words spoken in the book of the Forgotten Touch." Hilandra said. Mother and Hilandra left and made their way back to the palace. As they entered the throne room, Hilandra walked directly to this big old book.

"Mother, here is the book." Hilandra turned the pages to a passage that read.

"For those that seek the Deep Darkness it may be found within the resting place of the Bingjie. For it forms part of a Plain that is hidden. A place that could consume the Universe. There is a hidden object that can be used to wield the Kahul. A command spoken with serenity will give power to the chosen one. There lies darkness, but also light within these powers if you so dare." He continues, "The Deep Darkness can be controlled or it may just control thee."

"What does this mean" Mother asked.

"Where did you hear of this Kahul and Deep Darkness?" Hilandra asked Mother. She looks down at the pages in front of her and says, "From the darkness that lies deep within Lady Ciandra. She seeks the Kahul. She has no knowledge of it revealing itself to the Forgotten One. If she learns of what we know, she will try to find a way to the Bingjie to be able to seek its help to destroy the Forgotten One. But he is stronger than she thinks."

"Mother that Being is the destroyer of Realms. No Being through time has seen or faced the Bingjie. The Creators created the Bingjie to do their bidding."

"Yes Hilandra, but if Lady Ciandra uses her dark craft she will create warriors from the deep and stand with the Bingjie. She has not yet surrendered to the idea of overthrowing the throne. I must return to my Domain and prepare for the journey to Lady Salira. She might know of the command needed to wield the Kahul. The gathering of ceremony must be completed before the stars align."

"Yes Mother, we will wait for the one that cannot be named to return."

"I will leave at once." She stood back and stamps her Staff six times on the ground. A cloud of white smoke appears and she vanishes.

CHAPTER 9

ROAD TO THE BEGINNING

Princess Olia sensed Langos' return and sure enough, he was spotted leaving the woods. He made his way back to the house. I noticed Nana was not with him.

"Langos where is Nana?" I asked frantic.

"My Queen, please do not fear for Mother will return soon. There is a battle in Famos and Mother is the only Being that can face the Plunatra beast that Lady Ciandra is using in the battle."

"What? What is that?" I asked. Pat moved closely towards me to calm me down.

"Please my child. Nana knows how to handle this beast. She is Nature and I do believe she will be able to handle this Plunatra creature."

"My father Langos? What about him?" Olia asked trying to not show her worry.

"My Princess, the Prince is safe. His magnificent guards will protect him and the Beings of Famos but for now we will have to wait until Nana's return. Nana gave me passage to return and did not want me to be part of this battle."

"Okay Langos, all we have to do is wait on Nana to return so that she can tell us what happened and what will our next steps be." I said.

"My child, why don't you and Zack go for a walk in the garden and get some fresh air and when my blossom returns, Langos will call you."

"Okay Pat." We both agreed. Still feeling anxious, a walk would do us good, I thought. And we made our way out of the kitchen and to the gardens.

"Princess I can sense your inner light has faded and you should rest until Mother returns, for we do not know what news she will bring."

"Yes, Father. I will try to rest. I feel something is amiss, but I cannot say what. Perhaps it is because time is different in this Domain. I will need all my strength." Olia retired to her room. Pat and Langos walked to the porch where they made themselves comfortable to wait on Nana's return.

Time past and we were back at the house. We joined Pat and Langos on the porch.

"Uncle Pat, has Nana not come back yet?"

"Not yet my child, please come and sit. I do believe she will be back shortly."

"Okay Pat, but we will go and relax in the kitchen." Zack pulled out a chair and as we both sat down, a cloud of white smoke appeared in the center of the kitchen and with an instant Nana stood in front of us.

"Uncle Pat!" I yelled, and both him and Langos came running into the kitchen.

"My blossom, please sit down." Pat helped Nana with her cloak and Staff.

"Oh my dear, where is the Princess." Nana asked immediately.

"She is resting my blossom. Langos mentioned a battle?"

"Yes my dear, I am okay. But I bring with me sad news." Instantly Olia appeared. "Mother, what is this sadness I feel? My father? What has happened? I cannot see him in any of my visions."

"My child, I have terrible news. Your father our dear Prince Thelon, fought bravely on the battlefield." Olia fell to the ground in shock knowing full well that he did not make it. Pat rushed over to catch her and led her to a chair. Tears ran down her cheeks, turning into different colour crystals as she cried. Nana knelt in front of her and said,

"Do not weep my child. Your father's message to you was that he will always be with you. His wish was for the Queen to take her place so that the prophecy can be fulfilled."

"Yes Mother, my father feasts with the Kings and Queens of the past in the great light. I know his death will not be in vain for we will fulfill his last wishes. And when all is said and done, we will mourn his death."

"Yes my child. Your father was a brave Being and Lady Ciandra will answer for what she has done on this day." Nana stood up.

"What happen to the creature?" Langos asked.

"My son, I made sure that the beast obeyed me. I sent it back to where it came. Lady Ciandra is my concern because she is still consumed with the dark craft and escaped from the battle."

"Nana, what is this dark craft you speak of? This really concerns me." I asked.

"My child, there is no need for you or Zack to be concerned about this matter. Both of you have come so far and learnt a great deal of things in such a short time so please allow us to relax for now."

"The journey Nana, will we still have to take it? Or have things changed?" Zack asked.

"No, my son, nothing will affect our journey. My children, I know you have a lot of questions, but more will be made known to you once we enter the Domain of Lady Salira."

"Nana, when will we go on our journey?" I asked.

"My child, the wind will tell us. And only you will know."

"Why only me?"

"It will make itself known to only you in due time. Do not fret." I looked through the kitchen window and noticed the stillness in the air. I feel conflicted and anxious but I will wait calmly as Nana has suggested. I turned to Olia and said,

"I can feel your pain and I understand your grief. Perhaps you should try and get some rest. A deep sleep will help to preserve your strength and you may join us later."

"Yes my Queen. I think it will be good for me. I feel terribly weak." She got up and made her way to her room. There was a stillness in the atmosphere around us. You could not help but feel sad.

"Would anyone like some tea?" Zack offered.

"Yes, my son. That would be lovely." Nana responded. We sat silently as we sipped our tea before we started talking for almost an hour, when Langos made his way towards me and laid down. He started watching me closely as though he knew something was about to happen. I started humming a tune and everyone went quiet, listening to me. Nana turned to Pat and said,

"My dear, the manifestation. It has begun."

"My love, are you okay?" I couldn't hear Zack because I was in my own world and couldn't stop humming. The song I heard in my mind, only I could understand and it was so beautiful.

"My son, be calm. She hears the call of the wakening."

"Pat, I do not hear anything."

"Yes my son, only the Queen can hear her calling. We need to wait until the song has been completed to release her Inner Being, then we will start our journey." After a few minutes I stopped humming, and noticed everyone was watching me.

"What just happened? Did I fall asleep? I had such a wonderful dream. I was floating through water and felt so safe, then I woke up."

"My child, that was the song of the wakening. Only you could hear its call through the wind. It is time for us to start our journey." Nana said and Olia appeared.

"I see the Queen has heard her song."

"How do you know that Olia?" I asked.

"My Queen, I can see that your light is glowing brighter."

"What light? I cannot see anything." Zack said while looking at me.

"Zack, the Queens light will be shown to you momentarily."

"What must we wear Nana? For our journey?" I asked.

"My child, you will leave with the clothes you have on. You needn't worry about worldly things. You are needed most for our journey. Pat will pack in some treats for the road."

"Nana, what about the boys?" Zack asked.

"My son, no need to worry about them either. I have already put them in a deep sleep, you will be able to greet them, but they will only wake up when we return. Princess Olia will be here to protect and watch over them. That is the reason for her long deep sleep, to preserve her strength." Pat said and everyone started getting ready to leave. Zack and I made our way to the boy's bedroom and each gave them a kiss on their forehead and made our way to the porch. Nana got her cloak and Staff and joined Pat and Langos. Langos started glowing in a bright light and soon after it was over.

"The Shield has covered us for our protection. So that we may not be seen by the Creators. We can start making our way to the lake to see Lady Salira." Nana instructed. I did not say anything, or ask any questions, about the light we saw. As we walked towards the woods. Nana stopped, looking straight in front of her. We all stopped alongside her.

"Once we have crossed into the woods, Daina and Zack, do not look back. Olia will take care of the boys. Your future awaits." Nana stamps her Staff once and I could see little bright sparks appearing. We continued walking through the woods on the path that will lead us to the lake. The pathway we took, was bright with the morning light shining through the trees. The woods slowly came alive. With all the beautiful animals and the singing birds. The path seemed familiar and we were heading for the Big Tree. We turned off onto a very dull road, that seemed to have a lot of dead trees. No animals or birds in sight and I felt so much sorrow. Langos looked around and said,

"Mother, the darkness must have found a way through to this Domain when Dajeti was weak." I started to slow down and felt weak.

"What is this place?" I asked almost breathless. I felt as though I couldn't walk any further. Zack immediately grabbed my arm and said,

"Daina! Nana there's something wrong with Daina." Nana stopped and rushed over to me.

"My child, it is this darkness that you feel? Give me your hand." I stretched out my hand to her.

"Let us heal this place and vanquish this darkness. My child hold onto my hand I will guide your Inner Being to channel your light through me and with both our mystical power we will defeat this darkness." I held Nana's hand while everyone stepped back. She slowly lifted her Staff and a light formed around me. I lit up into a yellow bright light. Zack covered his eyes because of the brightness. The ground started to shake and a dome appeared to form. The darkness started to lift and the sun's rays broke through over these woods. The trees started to heal; flowers grew as the woods came back to life. Nana slowly pulled her Staff towards her and the dome disappeared. My light started to fade and eventually disappear. I felt restored.

"You see my child this is what you can do. You have the gift of healing." I looked around and could not believe what I had done. Zack was astonished.

"That was remarkable, my love." He took me in his arms and held me tight.

"I am so honoured to be your husband." I felt so safe in his arms.

"Thank you my dear, I am proud to call you my husband and the father of my children." I wished for this moment to never end.

"My children, we have to keep moving. The lake is still a distance to go. There is a marvelous place ahead where we will find rest." Suggested Pat. After a long walk we came across an open green field filled with flowers, that I have never seen before.

"My children, we will rest for a while before we carry on." Nana said. Zack took out a blanket, and I made myself comfortable. I noticed the grass and flowers moving though there was no wind.

"Nana, what is that? Something is moving."

"Yes, my love. I see it too, but what is it?" Zack added.

"My children since we left home, we have been protected by the Fixen. They are harmless creatures. Do not worry, they will make their presence known soon." Nana said as she continued,

"Thorpet, you may greet the Queen." A little voice could be heard but no-one could be seen.

"Oh Mother, I did not mean to scare anyone. Nor my people. We were merely curious to see the Queen and wanted to make sure her journey is going well." He said still hiding. I stood up and responded, "Who is speaking? Please show yourself." A small flower creature appeared and said,

"I am Thorpet my Queen, I do not mean you harm. If I may present my people my Queen." Little flower creatures appeared one by one, each with different names and gifts.

"These are my people and your humble servants; we have watched over you since childhood. We are your sworn protectors."

"Nana, they are adorable."

"They are indeed. But do not let that fool you, for they are valiant and fearless gifted creatures. A force not to be reckoned with."

"Okay Nana. Thorpet, you are very brave and I welcome you and your people on our journey."

"Thank you, my Queen." He said and little cheers filled the air.

"Zack, can you see them?"

"Yes my love. I have met them before, on our way back from the Forbidden Woods. They are strange little creatures." We all settled in and had a bite to eat. Langos moved closer to us, keeping an eye on me while I rested.

"Langos, are you okay my boy? I hope they didn't scare you; I think they are adorable, what do you think?"

"My Queen and Zack, I think Nana forgot to tell you. They have little sharp teeth." Langos said as Pat laughed.

"Langos?! Why do you want to frighten the children?"

"Father, but they do. Its okay, my Queen. They will not harm you. Zack however, I think you're sitting a bit too close to them." Zack turned to Thorpet and the little creature gave a wide smile and he could see two layers of razor-sharp teeth. He jumped up immediately.

"Langos, really? Why did you say that? And then made him smile?" Everyone including Thorpet broke out into laughter.

"Zack, I bet you never took Langos for the jokey type? Do not worry they will not bite." Nana said in her laughter. Some time had passed and Nana got up and said;

"My children it is time for us to make our way to the lake."

"Nana, how much further?" I asked.

"Close your eyes and listen, you will be able to hear the sounds of the lake." I closed my eyes and could see the lake in front of me.

"Nana I saw it."

"That is part of the gift you have." The place I saw looked amazing; the water was so clear. I cannot wait to get there. We packed up and started making our way to the lake. The Fixen disappeared into the flower field and kept a safe distance. I could not stop thinking of what I saw and started walking faster, out of pure excitement.

"My love, hold on. Not so fast, you're going to get tired." Zack called out to me.

"No my dear. I'm not sure where this strength is coming from, but I feel great."

"My blossom, please say something. I do not want her to burn herself out." Pat said with concern.

"She's drawn to the lake. Let her be. We're almost there, nothing will happen to her. Langos is right by her side." Soon after myself and Langos made it to the lake, with Zack following trailing right behind us. Standing close to the lakeside I could see two small boats with no sails or oars. Much like a canoe. Nana and Pat arrived a few minutes later.

"My children let us rest. The boats are here, but not ready for us to take our journey further." I slowly rubbed my tummy to see if she was awake. I felt a kick and found a place to sit down.

"My love, are you okay? I knew that fast walking was no good?" Zack said.

"Everything is okay, I wanted to know if she was still asleep. She just gave me a big kick, so that's a no." I replied happily.

"That is a relief. You had me worried for a second. Please don't do that again." Zack sat down next to me.

"Langos, when we leave, please do not leave Daina's side. Always stay close to her as will I."

"What are you so afraid of Zack?" I was a little irate.

"The only thing on this journey I cannot shake, is the fear of losing you. That is the reason why I asked Langos to always stay with you to protect you and our child."

"I understand. But do not fear, we're surrounded by family who will protect both of us."

"Okay my love." Zack said and Langos responded with a single nod. We sat for a little while longer until the sound of a trumpet was heard by all of us.

"My blossom, it is time. They are being announced." Pat said as he helped Nana on her feet.

"My children let us make our way to the boats." Nana said. She instructed myself, Zack and Langos to use one boat and her and Pat will use the other. Zack helped me to my feet and into the boat. Pat did the same for Nana and Langos got in last.

"Pat, how are we supposed to move? There are no sails or oars on the boat." Zack asked. And I wondered the same.

"You'll see." He said and the boats started to move by itself. We drifted towards a little Island in the middle of the lake and stopped.

"Nana, what's going on?" I asked.

"Relax. Everything will be fine." She said trying to reassure my nervous mind. When the boat stopped, it began to sink into the lake. I closed my eyes tight, clinging to Zack. He assured me that there is nothing to fear and I should open my eyes. I did just that. I noticed we were close to the bottom of the lake and still breathing normally.

"Nana, how is this possible that we are under water and can still breathe?" I asked.

"It is because of Langos' Shield that is making all this possible. Your gift also plays an important role." In the distance we could see a creature moving towards us.

"Great greetings my Queen. Protector. Shield. Mother and Father. I am Makton, Guardian of the Moeks. My Moenkis and I are here to be your guide to meet Lady Salira. The Lady awaits your presence and so will some of the other Moek clans."

"Greetings." We all responded.

"My Queen, there will be a small gathering tonight. Please follow me." He directed us on our watery path through the bottom of the lake. I could see many different creatures, filled with colour. I looked over to Nana and asked, "What are they? I have never seen fish like this before." Makton replied.

"My Queen, they are the deep dwellers of the Domain of Onasia. These creatures do not come close to the surface of any waters, not like the Moeks. We can live on land and in water. Although we prefer our own Domain. We are the Protectors of the Ocean, rivers and lakes of the Realm of Ekna.

"Children, we will be greeted in the Big Hall of Osangia in the Palace of Lady Salira and you will see many Moek tribes. When you see Lady Salira, she will bow to her knees and so will every Being present. Zack you needn't bow fully to your knees, you may bow your head in respect for the Queen. Once they have bowed, after a few minutes say the words; You May Resume Your Stand. My child, this is of great importance as the Queen to your Kingdom. Especially amongst the Moek tribes."

"Okay Nana." I said looking at Makton and thought what a strange looking Fish. He had long arms and legs with colorful fins and a beautiful long tail and I wondered what Lady Salira may look like. A beautiful sound coupled with singing caught my attention. It gave me goosebumps and I felt emotional while listening to it. I did not understand the meaning of what I heard.

"Zack, can you hear that?"

"Yes my love, its sounds like singing."

"Nana, can you hear that?"

"Yes my child we all can."

"I do not understand it." I had tears in my eyes.

"Makton please tell me, why do I feel this way? I am not sad, but I cannot stop my eyes from tearing up."

"My Queen, only the Moeks understand what they are singing. They are singing about the return of the Queen and the Child of Light. There are no words to describe the beauty my people sense within you my Queen, for you carry the Child of Destiny and that's what the song is about. The song is traveling through the waters of the Realm of Ekna. It is hidden from the Creators, that is why only the Moeks can understand the hidden language of song." He explained before continuing,

"My Queen, you must rest now, for we still have a long way to go before we arrive in the Osangia Palace. We are here to protect you all for there are hidden dangers in these waters. The Bingjie has his creatures that may cross over into our Domain, but they will not dare face us. So please rest." The tension in me eased up a little and I began to relax. Langos kept himself on high alert. Makton tried to convince him that there was no need to be on high alert because I was safe. He agreed to turn it down a notch, while still keeping an eye on me.

CHAPTER 10

THE MEETING OF REVEALING

"Mother we will be arriving at the Palace soon." Makton told Nana. In the far distance, lies a beautiful bright place.

"Oh my." I gasped.

"My Queen, we have arrived at the Osangia Palace in the Domain of Onasia. The Lady Salira will be waiting for you in the Big Hall. I will escort you, my Queen." As we approached the Palace, beautiful fishlike creatures glided around the surrounding waters. We stopped next to a walkway that was made of glass. It had a mirage effect, which looked like it may be moving slightly. Langos jumped out of the boat first, to show me that it was safe to walk on. Makton took me by the hand and led me out of the boat and the rest joined us on this strange walkway.

"My Queen, please follow me." Makton glided through the water towards me and led us into a big room filled with wonders no human eyes have ever seen before.

"My Queen, this is the Room of Remembrance. It is filled with items of the Moek clans. We have used during the centuries and as you can see, we are surface dwellers too. But that is no more, our people prefer the water." He said while pointing to some surface items. We walked towards a massive golden door with strange writing on it. It was magically beautiful. The closer we got, I could hear the trumpets in song, and the door opened.

"My Queen, I will announce you. Then you and your companions may enter." Makton glides forward and made the announcement.

"May I present to all Beings, Queen Liara. True heir to the Kingdom of Athela and Queen of all the Plains. Protector Zack. Shield Langos. Mother Nature and Father Time." As soon as he was finished, Makton moved out of the way quickly. As Lady Salira lifted her hand, Nana whispered to Zack and I, "My children that is the Lady." We nodded our heads and she said,

"Please, you may enter." I entered the room with Zack by my side. He kept my hand tightly and moved slowly down a few steps as a walking path made of red crystal stones appeared in front of us. The Moek Beings were on both sides of us and we could see Lady Salira standing waiting at the end of the path. When we reached the end, everyone started to bow; including Lady Salira. All the way down to their knees. Zack bowed his head. I looked across the room said,

"You May Resume Your Stand." Makton appeared and said,

"May I present to you Lady Salira. The Lady of the Lake and Protector of the Domain of Onasia."

"My Queen, I bid you and your companions welcome to our Domain. I hope you had a pleasant journey through the waters of Onasia."

"Yes, my lady, you have a beautiful Palace. and I would like to see more of this spectacular Domain."

"Yes my Queen, that would be an honor. We will have a gathering feast tonight in your honor my Queen. I have prepared chambers for you and your companions if you would may like to rest before our gathering." I smiled in agreeance as she continued. "My Queen, I am aware that you may have many questions, of which will be answered a little while later. But for now, please do make yourselves at home. We will discuss what is needed, first thing tomorrow morning."

"Yes, my lady. We will retire to our chambers until the gathering."

"My Queen, may I excuse myself? I do have some preparations that still need my attention. I would like to make your stay as rememberable as I can. Makton will accompany you and your travelers to your chambers." I nodded my head and said, "You may be excused." Lady Salira glided her way down a long passage and disappeared.

"My Queen, your chambers await." Makton lead us to a big room. The room was covered in a white glaze like frosting on a cake. Delicious.

"My Shield you may follow me." Makton said to Langos.

"Makton, Langos will be staying in our chambers."

"As you wish, my Queen." He bowed and left. Nana and Pat made their way to their chambers. Langos found a good spot, making himself comfortable to rest while we explored this magnificent room. There were different garments laid out for us on the bed.

"These are quite the clothes. I thought they might want to cover us in seaweed or fish skin." Langos broke out into laughter.

"I can agree with Zack. I never thought there would be clothes for us humans."

"My Queen, you will always be made comfortable. In the Domain of Famos, you will find it is not much different from the Onasia. My Queen, you and Zack need to rest. Time is different in this Domain, the waters of the lake can move fast or slow. So, it is best to get some rest before the celebration." Zack made his way to the bathroom to explore and discovered how spectacular it was. The bath was a giant seashell and the water flowed continuously.

"My love, come and see this incredible bath." I made my way to the bathroom and could see the magical water show unfolded in front of us.

"Langos, this is unbelievable!"

"Yes, my Queen. The Kingdom of Athela is a magical place." We all walked back to the bedroom, made ourselves comfortable and dozed off for quite some time.

A knock at the door woke Zack and I immediately. I wonder who that could be?

"Who is there?" I asked and from the other side of the door we could hear a voice saying,

"It's Nana and Pat. May we come in?"

"Oh yes." I said. They entered and were just as amazed at our room as we were.

"Nana is it time already? We do not want to miss the celebration."

"No, my child. You are the guest of honor; it is impossible to miss your own celebration. We came to check in on how everyone is doing. I think you could start getting ready. The celebration will start soon."

"Nana, I have to say you and Pat do look exquisite for the celebration." Zack added.

"Oh my son, we received garments for this evening as well. I feel honored to be part of this welcoming event." I got up out of bed and showed Nana the dress that was laid out for me to wear for the evening.

"What a beautiful dress. It is fit for a Queen. Compliments your eyes as well. Zack you will look dashing in your suit. That's fit for a King. We will excuse ourselves and make our way to the Big Hall until you are ready to join us."

Zack and I got dressed and made our way to the celebration. An announcement was made presenting us to those that did not witness our arrival. We entered the hall, and everyone rose and bowed. I thought to myself, this feels strange but also good.

"My Queen, please be seated in the royal chair that was made especially for you." Lady Salira said as she ushered Zack to a seat next to me. She stepped back and bowed her head. She made her way to her seat at the other end of the table. The Moek clan joined her in standing while Zack and I remained seated with Langos by my side. She raised her glass and said,

"Today we are all gathered here to bear witness to a miracle that was bestowed upon us. An inspiration for life and to know the Child of Light is in our presence. I sense the miracle flowing through our Queen. The Child of Light is the beacon to us all and will be born when the prophecy is fulfilled. I welcome you all, to the Domain of Onasia. Let the celebration begin!" Everyone bowed their heads, cheered thereafter and sat down. I leaned over to Nana and asked,

"Lady Salira's speech was a bit confusing, what did she mean?"

"As it should be, because you are not there yet. It is difficult to explain when you are not ready to understand, but soon you will be." I nodded my head in anticipation and decided to let it go and enjoy myself. Zack joined us at the table. He was quickly distracted by the feeling that someone was watching him. He then heard Lady Salira speak to him telepathically.

"I can see what you possess in my Domain. It is filled with darkness, yet it holds light too."

"Yes, I know. I need guidance." Zack turned to face Lady Salira and spoke out loud in response to what she said and everyone went quiet.

"My son, are you okay? Who are you talking too?" Nana asked.

"Lady Salira. Did you not hear her Nana?"

"No, my son. She spoke to you alone." Right, Zack thought feeling a little embarrassed. I could sense Zack was still in shock that Lady Salira spoke to him using her mind, I reassured him that everything Nana said was true and he needn't worry. He lifted his glass of water towards Salira and she nodded her head in acknowledgement.

The celebration continued with singing, dancing and feasting. I was introduced to several Beings and I was told about the different languages the Moek tribes spoke. I was fascinated with what I saw. Langos kept a watchful eye on all of us, especially me. He paid close attention to Zack and noticed that he had a lot on his mind. Lady Salira glanced at Zack on occasion, and Langos knew that she had the gift of sight. She is also one of the few that could sense the Kahul. I respect him for not dropping his guard, especially at a time like this. He slowly made his way to me and sat down.

"So Langos, you promised me you will show me your true self once we see Lady Salira. Why are you still in a dog form?"

"My Queen, the time is close."

"I am excited to see your true form, but I still like the way you are now." Pat and Nana glanced at the table and saw there were a few Moeks who did not seem too keen with my arrival. They decided not to voice their opinion. They looked at each other without saying a word. Langos started sensing a dark unnatural feeling. He turned to Nana and said,

"Mother, how much longer will this celebration be? I can sense the Queen is getting really tired." I was surprised at what Langos insinuated.

"Langos I am not that tired." Zack knew immediately what Langos meant.

"My love, I think it's time for us to retire. We have a busy day ahead of us tomorrow." Nana and Pat both agreed.

"Yes Zack, I think you and Langos should take the Queen to go rest. It is the best thing for her at this moment."

"Okay, Nana." I said and as I got up, Lady Salira joined our conversation.

"My Queen, I hope you have a good night's rest."

"This was a wonderful celebration thank you." Zack took me by the hand with Langos following behind after we greeted everyone, and off we went to our chambers. I stopped midway and asked, "What is going on with the both of you? Why are you acting so strange?" Langos looked around and said,

"My Queen, please may we get you to your chambers and I will answer your question."

"Yes my love, let's get you to your room first." And we made our way to the chambers. Langos entered the room first to see if the coast was clear. He then called Zack and told him that we could enter.

"Langos, what is going on? Why are you and Zack acting so weird? Are you up to something?"

"My love, when Lady Salira spoke to me telepathically, I got a terrible feeling."

"Zack you should know, Lady Salira fears the Kahul of Darkness. It is clear to me now that she knows more than what she is letting on. But do not fret, I will gather as much intel as I have to before we go any further on our journey." Langos informed Zack.

"Why did we have to leave the celebration so soon, I was enjoying myself."

"My Queen, when we entered this Domain, I sensed there was a hidden presence not familiar to me when we arrived. There were some of the Moek clans that were not pleased with your arrival. I know Mother and Father also sensed it. I am your Shield my Queen and I could sense your life was in danger. And that is why we left. You are safe now and safe from the Creators. But not from the darkness that lies in this Domain." Langos explained. "The darkness I sensed could only have come from the Bingjie's Domain."

"Langos, what about Lady Salira, is she also infected with this darkness?"

"No, my Queen. Lady Salira has not been infected. We do not know how many of the Moek clans have been filled with this darkness." Langos continued our discussion while Nana and Pat stayed behind. They had a feeling that everything was not as it should be. Lady Salira was not herself. As the night went on, fewer clans were sitting at the table. And some of them were not as friendly as they were before. Lady Salira did not want to involve herself with the conversations among clans. The Finosh clan of the Moeks, started bickering about politics. Lady Salira then excused herself and bid everyone a good night. Makton was left in charge to see the rest of the guests off. Nana and Pat also excused themselves and retired for the night. There was a knock at our door. Zack got up and asked, "Who is there?"

"My son, it is Nana and Pat. May we come in?"

"Yes Nana, please do." He opened the door.

"My children, we came to check on you and to say goodnight."

"Mother, what haunts this place? I can sense darkness within these waters?" Langos asked concerned.

"Yes my son, we have felt it too. We saw the squabbling and darkness in some of the Clans. I fear Lady Salira is in great danger. Please my children, be cautious of the Moeks tomorrow. I fear this place is not like it used to be."

"They seemed delighted to see us. They were pleasant towards me." I said.

"Yes, my child. Lady Salira made sure that she kept the dark ones away from you, because she knew you will sense those that are not good. My children, tomorrow is a big day. We need to get some rest."

"Nana I need to speak to Lady Salira. I know she has knowledge of the Kahul. And she knows more than she's letting on." Zack claimed.

"Yes, my son. We will speak to Lady Salira tomorrow. Get some rest." And they said good night and left.

Langos sat up when he sensed someone was close to their door. He knew it was neither Nana nor Pat. He opened the door and it was Makton.

"My Shield, Lady Salira has requested that the Queen and all her companions join her in her chambers early in the morning. Please do not speak of this to anyone beside those who traveled on the boat to this Domain. I will call you in the morning. I bid you a good night." And he left. As Langos returned into the room, I asked; "Who was that Langos?"

"My Queen, it was Makton. Lady Salira has requested for us to join her early in the morning at her chambers." I looked at Zack and said,

"That sounds a bit strange. But yes Langos, we will go."

"Yes, my Queen. Makton will call for us in the morning. My Queen and Zack, I do ask one thing."

"Yes, Langos we are listening."

"Please do not leave this room until we are called." We agreed to what Langos requested. I turned to Zack and said,

"That includes no exploring or wandering off if you get bored or can't sleep. I hope that is clear enough?"

"Not in this place. It's a little creepy. I am staying right here in this room all night. I don't feel like being eaten by some strange thing." We all said our good nights and turned off the light.

The room started glowing with a blue colour and beautiful sounds could be heard coming from the lake. It was soothing, and I started to drift off. I could feel my child becoming restless. I spoke to her as I rubbed my tummy.

"My girl please settle down. I know time seems different in this Domain, but I would like both of us to sleep well for I do not know what we might have to face tomorrow." I felt a familiar warmth running through me and saw Langos approach my bedside.

"My Queen, I am here and will stay right next to you, so both of you can rest." It felt as though his words hypnotized me and I fell asleep immediately.

The sound of the lake was all I heard the next morning as I woke and saw Zack not in bed. I scanned the room.

"Oh, there you are my dear. I got a fright when you were not next to me, are you alright?"

"Yes, my love. Good morning." He said, "I hope you slept well?"

"Yes, I feel well rested." I made my way to the bathroom to get ready for the day and there was a knock at the door.

"May we come in? It's Nana and Pat."

"Yes please do." Zack replied.

"Morning everyone, hope that you are all well rested. Where is Daina?" They asked.

"She's in the bathroom, getting ready for the day." Zack responded. "It seems we have all been summoned to Lady Salira's chambers this morning."

"Yes, my child. We were told by Makton last night as we left your chambers." Pat said.

"Good morning Nana and Pat. I hope you had a good night's rest. This place is so peaceful, I could hear the sounds of the lake while sleeping. It was such a soothing sensation. Except for the little one." I said as I rubbed my tummy.

"She was a bit restless last night. Thanks to Langos, I eventually fell asleep." I was all dressed and ready to go.

"Yes my child. I too could not sleep very easily last night. The darkness in this place was felt by us all including your child. Langos' light made her and you feel safe. That is why both of you fell asleep eventually." That made sense, I thought. "Lady Salira will call on us soon." Nana said, and there was a knock on the door.

"You may open Zack, it is Makton I believe." Nana proposed. He made his way to the door and opened it. And indeed, it was Makton. He turned to face Nana and nodded his head.

"You may come inside." Nana said, and Makton walked towards me and bowed.

"My Queen. Greetings to you and all. Lady Salira has requested your company at her chambers. May I guide the way?"

"Yes, Makton, you may." We walked through the Palace hallways that seemed quiet. Further down the passage we heard whispering and soft talking, echoing down the hallway. I could not see who or where it came from. I held onto Zack's hand tightly, and Langos was right by my side on high alert. When we finally arrived at Lady Salira's chambers and it was a relief for us all. We stood in front of these big, beautiful doors and it magically opened.

"Greetings my Queen and to all." Salira said,

"Please come in." We made our way to a round table, filled with food and drinks.

"Make yourselves comfortable, and enjoy your meal." We all sat, and the doors closed. Makton stood in front of the doors and kept guard.

"My Lady, I sense a weakness in you. You seem consumed with powers that is beyond your control in this Domain."

"Mother, if I may. I do not want to burden the Queen at this moment." Langos looked at Salira and sensed that she was filled with fear. I stood up and walked to Salira.

"My Queen, it is I who will come to you, if you so wish."

"No my Lady." I took her hand. "Please tell me what troubles you. We are here to help. I do know there is a darkness in this place and we can sense it. But you have to tell us so we can help." Lady Salira offered for me to sit down.

"My Queen, for centuries the Moeks have lived in peace. But for the last few weeks my people have become different. Filled with greed and jealousy. My clans are peaceful Beings, but something has changed in them and I have no control over it. I have been told by the Seer's of Onasia that it comes from the waters of the Bingjie, and the Svewils have been spotted in the Outer Domains. They are the Guardians of the Bingjie, they are filled with darkness. Some of my fellow Beings have come into contact with the Svewils and that was when they started to change."

"My Lady, what can you tell us about the Kahul of Darkness? I have been told a few stories about it but I am still not well versed on the matter." Zack asked insanely curious to know.

"I do know you are the Keeper of the Kahul and it will only answer to you. For in the Book of Legends of Onasia, I have read that one day the purest of hearts will have to face the Bingjie in the Big Battle of Depth. There is a command that must be spoken to wield the Kahul from Darkness into Light. The Purest will be given two alternatives; destroy or forgive and that will not be easy. For the Bingjie is cunning and willful.

He will try to trick the chosen one to win them over into the darkness."

"My Lady, what is the command? I do not want to hurt this creature, although I am told that I need to defeat him. I also do not want to destroy anything or anyone. All I want is to have my child born safely in the Palace of Famos. Please give me guidance, that is all I ask."

"Zack, you are pure of heart. But you will do well to be wary of the Bingjie's cunning ways. The command you need to speak, only the Bingjie knows. I believe you will find a way to get the Bingjie to reveal it to you." I could tell that Zack took in every word she said seriously.

"Zack, Makton and his **Moenkis** will join you in the battle that you must face. You will need to devise a tactical plan to face the Svewil army so that you can get close to the Bingjie's doorway." Lady Salira walked towards a small draw, pulled out a map and opened it on the table. We all moved closer to see the map.

"This is the map of the waters that lead to the Bingjie's Domain." She pointed to show the layout and Makton said,

"Yes my Lady we need to plan with Protector Zack and Shield Langos on how the battle should commence." I thought to myself, 'what do we know of battles and strategies.'

"My Queen, Zack is a warrior full of strength and wisdom that neither you nor I know of. Please forgive me for reading your thoughts. I had to emphasize his capabilities."

"I agree with you. And please you do not need to ask for forgiveness Lady Salira."

"I will call my greatest warrior. He knows these waters well my Lady." Makton said. The doors opened and a Moenkis warrior appeared.

"My Queen, my Lady and all. You summoned me."

"Yes, there is a lot of work to be done. Please join us." She said. He entered and we all sat and discussed the best tactical plan.

CHAPTER **11**

BATTLE OF THE BINGJIE

The planning of the battle started to take shape. It slowly fell into place. While the discussions continued in the Palace of Osangia, Lady Ciandra joined her Trimos warriors in the Dark Woods. The woods lie close to a hidden passage that only the banished Seer Trogno from the Trimos Domain had knowledge of. He then past the knowledge of the secret location onto Ciandra. Her dark powers allowed her to see a glimpse of the future. However, her abilities were weakened by Mother Nature during the battle in Famos. The energy she used had exhausted her power. She was unable to modify her Trimos warriors for the battle that may arise in the waters of Onasia. She assembled her warriors and said,

"I, Lady Ciandra your leader will seek the Great Bingjie and will use the Ipmant tongue to speak the mightiest command to the great beast. I have seen that I, your leader will fight side by side with the great mighty dark warriors of the Bingjie. We will destroy those who stand in my way to become Queen of this Kingdom, and Queen of all. This I swear to you! I will not rest until I have claimed this Kingdom! For I believe that the throne was not only meant for royal blood but for any Being, and that Being will be me. I will leave you and offer my obedience to the Bingjie. For he will become my mighty beast!" The Trimos warriors cheered in a great uproar and as loud as they possibly could.

"I will start my journey and return as your Queen." She walked towards the lake and entered the dark waters. She spoke the dark craft tongue and submerged herself into the water. She moved through the water past deep trenches filled with piercing eyes but did not fear anything, for the darkness within her protected her from any dark Being except the Bingjie. Time passes and Ciandra came upon a cave where the waters were so evil, that it filled her with fear unrecognisable even to her. A voice from the cave, started speaking to her.

"Ciandra, I have sensed you in my Domain. Your dark craft feeds my power and for that you have no power over me, little Trimos. I can see the fear within you. For I am the Bingjie and you are nothing." He said. Ciandra replied instantly with a loud squeaky voice.

"Great and all Powerful Mighty Bingjie, the highest Being filled with darkness. I, Lady Ciandra, wish to offer you my dark craft to join you in fulfilling my destiny."

"Ciandra, your destiny! You have no destiny. You were born a Being of the Trimos clan, who are you to speak of destiny?" He slowly moved towards her with his intense yellow eyes that glowed in the darkness. She started moving backwards and noticed there were hundreds of red eyes staring back at her.

"Why so fearful, Ciandra? I thought you were here to join me with your turpitude demeanour, or allow my Svewils to feast on you. All this talk has woken me from my rest. I will now give you to my Svewils.

"Please great Bingjie. Hear me. I have learnt about the Princess of Athela that is with child who seeks passage through your Domain. I do foresee there might be a battle in these waters. I do request to join you if the battle arises, and wish to lead your army."

"Ciandra, what you speak of, I have seen. I am the great one and I can see further then your dark craft. I am aware of Prince Thelon's death by your hand. Yet still you were defeated by Mother Nature in the Domain of Famos. So, tell me why should I allow you to join me? I the great one, will destroy this human they call Zack. I know he laid claim to the Kahul and I also know he lacks the wisdom to wield it. For that I will destroy him.

"Oh no, Great Bingjie. The Yungnas and Lady Salira might have the wisdom of this object. Let me lead your army Great Bingjie. I will destroy this human Zack, in the same way I did with Prince Thelon, but only in the open dark waters of your Domain. I will set you free to roam the open waters of Onasia when I become Queen of Athela." The Bingjie laughed at her notion.

"You Trimos? Queen? You are not of royal descent. Yet you speak of setting me free? You know not how. One thing I do desire is to make a meal of Lady Salira and destroy those Moeks from Osangia. My darkness has infected some of the Moeks. If a battle were to commence, I will call upon them to join my Svewils. Ciandra, I will let you lead my army. On condition that you destroy the human before he finds a way through my Svewils."

"My Great Binjie, I will not fail you. Once I have defeated this Zack, I will destroy the Princess and her child." Excitement filled her eyes as she spoke maliciously,

"I cannot wait for this battle to commence." Ciandra and the Bingjie broke out into a terrifying laugh that could be felt through the waters of Onasia.

"Go now Ciandra. I will summon my army to follow you as their leader. Prepare for battle."

"Yes Great Bingjie, I will." She returned to the water and the Svewils followed her. Their laughter echoed through the waters of the lake and the Seer Lonkel of the Moek clan, rushed to Lady Salira's chambers. The doors opened and he yelled in panic.

"My Queen, my Lady and all." He greeted before continuing. "I have felt the evil from the Bingjie through the waters. I have seen Lady Ciandra found a way to the Bingjie's lair and has joined him for the battle yet to come.

"Please Lonkel. Do not fear what you have sensed or seen. We are preparing for the battle you speak of."

"My Lady, I will inform the other Seers. We will prepare for what may come." He said and left.

"Today is the day the battle will commence." Nana said.

"My Lady, I will call upon the Moenkis army to prepare for battle. We will face the battle with might and strength. I believe in the human Zack and Shield Langos to find a way through the battleground for Protector Zack to face the Bingjie." Makton declared boldly. Lady Salira walked towards a cupboard and took something out of a glass box. It looked like a suit covered with white shiny fish scales.

"Zack please step forward. On this day of battle, I present to you the Armour of Finoktin. This is not a suit for just anyone. Only the Forgotten One will be accepted as its master. It will gift you with gliding, and it will protect you as it guides you through the waters of the Svewils. Remember Zack you must remain calm and collected, for the Svewils sense fear. Once Langos has shown you a pathway through the Svewils, call upon the Bingjie. He will appear, for he knows you are coming. Do not be fooled by him, for he has to invite you into his evil waters. There you will be able to wield the Kahul. But do not forget, he has to invite you in. The Bingjie will try and trick you."

"Yes my Lady, I understand. I will keep my fear at bay." She took the suit out of the glass container. It coasted around the room and appeared to be changing into different colours. We all stared in awe at the beauty of the suit's performance. Right before it stopped in front of Zack, hovering like a nervous man on his wedding day. And then it stopped completely. Charging directly for Zack as it moulded itself to his body. Zack was left in complete shock as he turned to me and said. "Oh my, that felt amazing!" He leaped into the air, "I feel invisible." He said.

"Calm down Zack. You need to get used to the suit."

"Yes Zack, I agree with our Queen. The Finoktin Armour is bound to you for life. The Armour was magically created into a lifeform by the old Seer's of Onasia. It was predicted that one day the Forgotten One will claim the armour to face a dark force. Be good to it Zack and it will protect you for life."

"Yes my Lady, I will." Zack responded in agreeance.

"It is time for you all to start your journey. My Queen, I bid you safe passage. We will all meet again soon." She bowed and the chamber doors opened.

"My Queen. Please follow me." Makton addressed everyone in the room. We made our way to the boats and witnessed rows of Moenkis warriors getting ready for battle. As we walked, I kept Zack's hand tightly.

"My love, don't worry. Everything will work out just fine. With this armour and the Kahul, I will defeat the Bingjie so we can enter the Palace safely".

"Oh Zack, I really miss the boys and hope everything goes well for all of us. I do have faith in you." Makton stops next to the boat and takes my hand to help me climb into the boat. The rest followed suit.

"My Queen, you will all travel in one boat. These waters have hidden dangers but do not fear my Queen. My Moenkis and I will protect you. I will leave some Moenkis to guard you and the Yungnas, my Queen." Once everyone has settled, the boats started moving. I could feel that my baby was settled and quiet. I noticed the tension in everyone around me except Zack, he was very calm and relaxed. Langos kept looking around making sure there was no danger ahead. I found comfort on Zack's shoulder as he held my hand tight in response. He could sense I was a little worried but decided not to say anything. The water life around us was beautiful and unlike anything I have ever seen. The waters were clear and blue, and then appeared darker in the distance.

"My Shield, this is as far as the boat will travel." Makton informed Langos. "The Queen and the Yungnas will be safe in this location. We will follow the current, as it will lead us to colder waters and the colour of the water will become darker.

There we will find the Bingjie's Domain." I turned to Zack and Langos, gave each one a hug and a kiss.

"Zack my love, please be safe. I will always be with you in spirit. Langos protect yourself, both of you should come back to us unharmed. We will wait for your safe return." Nana and Pat greeted them as well.

"You are my son's; I know you will succeed in your fight." Nana continued. "Zack, remember when you are surrounded by the darkness and feel afraid, you can always call upon your child to give you light amidst the darkness." Zack and Langos greeted everyone while Makton called out to his warriors to follow and they left. Langos could sense the child through Zack as he saw the light within him. They could see the boat in the far distance, the water temperature changed and it became murky.

"Zack, this is the point where you should clear your mind. As we move further, we will get closer to the Svewils." Langos said to Zack.

"Yes." Zack responded as he moved through the water. No life forms were visible. He thought to himself, 'this is no place for anything to live, what could survive here? It looks like a graveyard, but without the dead.' Makton calls out to the Moenkis warriors and they glided through the water ahead of Zack and Langos, to where the water became darker. In the distance Makton could see a big army of Svewils and some of the Finosh clans hovering with Lady Ciandra, waiting in anticipation. He called for formation and the warriors moved into position. Zack and Langos remained out of sight. They could see that they were outnumbered and probably out matched.

"Courage, Zack. Just have faith, believe in yourself and this will all be over soon. So, let's get this Bingjie." Zack told himself silently. Makton moved back towards Langos and Zack.

"I will move my warriors forward and when they attack, Langos, you need to find a pathway through the battlefield for the Protector. Zack past this battlefield, you will find a wall of Svewils. You will need to move carefully through these creatures, do not awake them or they will attack. Once you are past these creatures you only have a few minutes to call the Bingjie. You will know what to do from there on." He said. Makton and the Moenkis moved forward and Lady Ciandra called out to her army, "Destroy them all! Leave the human to me."

"Attack!!" Makton gave the order to keep a close circle formation because he knew the Finosh tactics in battle. Their long razor-sharp tails could not penetrate the skin of the Moenkis as they lashed out. They drew their swords and chopped off their tails. However, minutes later it grew back.

"What is this?" A warrior called out,

"This is dark magic." He said. Makton immediately shouted, "Press forward and keep fighting! For today no warrior of mine will fall!" Zack and Langos kept safe in the centre to find a clear way for Zack to pass. Lady Ciandra fought hard trying to break through the closed formation, but the Moenkis did not break form. Part of the Svewils moved in for the battle as Makton called out to Langos, "Your time is now or never, these creatures approaching will break through our hold, Zack you need to get to the Bingjie's doorway when you call upon it, only then will the Svewils stop and go back into a deep sleep." Langos showed Zack an opening that he could use. Ciandra and her army were preoccupied with the fight.

"Zack, the Svewils that are lying dormant will not attack you unless you touch them. Be careful." Langos said. He saw an opening and his armour made him invisible, he quickly moved through the battlefield undetected. As he got closer, to what he thought was a wall, was thousands of little flat looking creatures with tentacles all curled together. It seemed as though, all of them were staring at something in the distance with their big black eyes and sharp little teeth. 'So, they are the Svewils, ugly looking creatures.' He thought. 'I need to find a way through them. No one mentioned anything about tentacles, this makes it much more difficult. Okay Zack, this suit will guide me. I must be careful not to touch any part of them.' Zack sees an opening, but couldn't go further. The suit would not allow him. The Svewils changed their position and still he could not move. He waited for a few seconds and the suit started moving him forward. Entering the Svewils, he could see they were still in a deep trance and did not notice him. In the distance, he could see a massive doorway. As he got closer his right foot touched a tentacle. All the Svewils turned towards him. Their eyes turned red indicating an attack mode and showing their teeth. They started swarming him, biting into his suit trying to rip through to his flesh. He tried to fight them off and suddenly they stopped. Zack found himself in front of a black door. Zack turned around and noticed that all the Svewils became dormant, including the one's on the battlefield approaching the Moenkis warriors. Lady Ciandra saw Zack in front of the door. She tried to reach him, but it was too late. The Svewils started hovering together, like they were waiting for something. He turned to face the door once more and it opened.

Zack sees a dark shadow. The Svewils squeaked with fear and Zack had to cover his ears. It was a tormenting sound. He could feel a gust of wind pass him and the Svewils went back into their gazing stance. Zack heard a voice coming from the other side of the doorway but still could only see a shadow as it spoke.

"We meet again little man. Just look at you! You are not worthy to bleed in my waters. You are useless. Do you think you may just enter my Domain? You worthless little human. I am much more powerful than you are. Do you think because you have the Kahul of Darkness that you can defeat me, the Great All Powerful Bingjie? I will let my Svewils feed on you then I will send you into the dark Forgotten Plain, where you will suffer forever. I am waiting. Come destroy me. You will never see your so-called Queen and children again! Why so quiet? I can smell your fear." Zack stood his ground, and listened to the creature as it tried to put fear into him. The Bingjie came closer to its doorway and it showed part of itself to Zack. It was enormous. Covered in spikes, big yellow glowing eyes and flashing tentacles moving around as it hovered in the water. Its mouth was enormous, filled with razor-sharp teeth with a snake-like tongue.

"You human called Zack. I can taste your fear, why don't you come closer? You are a small man, come closer." He spoke with a hissing sound. Zack kept his distance because he knew the Bingjie was trying to lure him and attack him.

"No beast! I will not enter unless you invite me in."

"Human, you bore me to death."

"Bingjie, if you give me safe passage, I will spare you. But if not, I will destroy you and all your followers.

"Ha, Ha, Ha! You destroy me? Never! No-one can destroy me!" Zack noticed around him that the Svewils were still in their trance position and the Moenkis were holding their ground. He kept an eye on the Svewils in case they attack again. He turned towards the Bingjie,

"Okay beast. I am only human, so why not invite me in? Do you fear me?"

"The all Powerful One fear you? Alright, I invite you to come in but here I will finish you. You may enter."

"I accept your invitation Bingjie." He started gliding through the doorway. The Bingjie disappeared into the dark waters. As Zack moved around, he could see red and green eyes appearing in the distance around him.

"Beast. Show yourself! Why hide in the dark waters?" Zack could feel that there was something in the waters around him, but not touching him. He looked around, but could not see what he felt. Small shadows appeared around him. He thought to himself, 'Courage Zack, you can defeat anything.'

"Little man! My Shadow-Rawer's seem to like the scent of human. They have never had human before, but today they will feast on you."

"Bingjie, I do not have time for your games. Face me or fear me! But stop trying to frighten me. I do not fear you Bingjie nor your Shadow-Rawers, show yourself!" He shouted. Zack felt something swim past him and tried to tear his suit but to no avail. The Bingjie started moving closer to Zack while exposing its full form. Zack felt a little fear, but tried not to show it.

"I call upon the Kahul of Darkness to become the Kahul of Light as it is revealed." Zack shouted at the top of his lungs. The Kahul appeared on Zack's right hand. A light shined so bright that Zack could see the Bingjie feared it, as it backed off from him.

"You little man, you cannot wield the Kahul. Do you think I will give you the command to use it against me? Never!"

"Bingjie, I command you give me the words for I will annihilate you if you do not! I have the power within me to do so." The Bingjie moved closer to Zack and said,

"I do not fear you or your light!" The Bingjie rushed for Zack in the hopes of scaring him, but he showed no fear. Zack thought of different ways to get the beast to divulge the words of command, thinking about what Nana said. Zack stood still in the water, closed his eyes and spoke in his mind to me.

"My love, I need you and our baby's strength. Please let my light shine brighter, I need both of you. I feel lost in this dark place, for this beast does not fear anything. The darkness I can feel is feeding on my strength." As Zack opened his eyes, he felt something strange graze his leg followed by a sharp pain. The Bingjie moved swiftly towards Zack and lashed out one of his tentacles covered in spikes and pierced his right arm. Zack could feel the pain rushing through his body, making him paralyzed as he faintly closed his eyes. The Bingjie broke out in laughter, as he could see the water surrounding them fill with Zack's blood.

"Yes little human, your end is near." As Zack floated around lifelessly in the water, he could feel himself fading, and just then he heard a voice.

"Papa, I am here with you. Do not fear what you see or feel. I will give your inner spirit strength to heal your wounds." Her voice was like a distant memory to him.

"Papa!" She shouted, "Wake up!" And suddenly Zack opened his eyes and he knew it was his little girl. He could feel her power coursing through him. The Bingjie was taken by surprise to see Zack still alive. He stood up and looked straight at the Bingjie.

"What kind of magic is this?" The Bingjie asked.

"Why are you not dead? My poisons should be coursing through your pathetic human body and you should be no more." Zack still staring at the Bingjie gave no answer. The Bingjie started to glide back away from Zack into the darkness of the water. Zack started to concentrate on what needed to be done to get the words of command from the Bingjie and his child spoke to him again.

"Papa, the beast thinks he is wise. Ask this question, I know he will fail in answering. What will be my given name? If it calls out the wrong name, then it must disclose the words of command. Remember, Papa it is cunning and will try and trick you. But it will not succeed because I am with you." Zack looked around and called out courageously.

"Bingjie, you claim you are Powerful and wise. I have one question for you." The Bingjie moved closer to him.

"Yes human. What do you want? Before I start chewing on you."

"If you give the right answer to my question, then you may do so. But if not, you must give me the command."

"Oh little human, why should I do that? If I can eat you now." Zack thinks quickly and says, "But are you not the most Powerful creature? What will one question be to you?"

"Alright, little man. What is your question?"

"Bingjie, if you are wrong, how do I know you will keep your word?"

"You may ask. I will keep my word; you are an interesting human. I can taste your flesh. Now ask!" Zack could sense the Bingjie's annoyance.

"Bingjie the all-knower of things. My question is; what will my unborn child's name be?"

"Her name? Oh human, that is too easy. She will be named after her grandmother Liaana. But she will never be born." He said. "I am right, I know." Zack moved around and the little voice said.

"No Papa, he is wrong. My name will be Evelyn. The creature is wrong."

"No Bingjie, you are wrong. I command you, to give me the words of command."

"Never human! You are trying to trick me." The water that surrounded Zack started moving rapidly. He starts spinning and is thrown around like a rag doll.

"No Bingjie! You said you will keep your word!"

"Never!" He shouted. The waters suddenly stop. Zack froze and a light shined through him as his daughter spoke.

"Bingjie, give us the words of command or you will be no more!" The creature cowered down knowing it was not Zack but his unborn child that spoke through him. He cowardly says, "I will tell you the words of command, and then I will be no more. What will you be named?" He asked. But the little princess did not fall for his cunning ways and demanded he tell them what Zack needed to know. The Bingjie glides away from Zack and says, "The command is *Bing Tack Svew*." Zack still shining bright with light said, "I call in the name *Bing Tack Svew*, the Kahul of Light," Zack turns his hand to the Bingjie. "I, the Forgotten One, command you and your creatures from the dark to accept me as your master and to release all the

Moeks that you have filled with darkness. You and your creatures will flee deep into the darkness of this domain. You will go into a deep sleep, until the day I call upon you." With the markings on his hand and arm standing boldly, the Bingjie responded.

"I accept your command, Forgotten One and will wait until the day we meet again." The Bingjie, slowly disappears followed by his red and green-eyed creatures, into the deepest darkest pit. Zack felt relieved. He looked around and noticed Svewils were gone. The Moenkis cheered when they saw Zack emerge from that dark place. Langos made his way towards Zack and said,

"I will call on Mother to join us."

"What happened to Lady Ciandra?" Zack asked.

"When you entered the doorway of the Bingjie, she abandoned her army, fled into the dark waters and vanished."

"Okay, good Langos. Hopefully soon we will be able to capture her and lock her away for good."

"I will go meet Mother and the rest, and bring them to you." Langos said and left. I witnessed Zack's victory through the light of our child.

"Nana, it's over, Zack did it!" I exclaimed.

"I know, my child. I can hear Langos' thoughts. We can make our way to them now." Nana calls to the Moenkis warrior that was protecting us and informs him that they won the battle. And we are free to join the rest of the group.

"We may proceed."

"As you wish Mother." The warrior responded. We moved through the waters to where Langos awaits us.

"My Queen this is as far as the journey carries me and my warriors. You are safe now. Langos will guide you further. I bid you safe journey until we will meet again." Makton said as he bowed. Nana and Pat could sense the darkness of Onasia was lifted and that Lady Salira was safe.

"My Queen, this way. Zack is waiting for us. We will have safe passage, but we must hurry." Langos showed us the way to Zack. I felt over joyed and excited to see that he was safe. I could also see he was hurt.

"Zack, you're hurt."

"Oh my love, it is just a scratch. I will live."

"No it seems the Bingjie's venom is still coursing through you and it may become fatal. Your unborn child could not fully heal you in these dark waters. So please, if I may, I will heal you." Langos said and blew over Zack, and his wounds healed.

"Thank you." Zack said and took me in his arms.

"All will be okay my love. We can now complete our journey." I held onto Zack with a tight grip because I was filled with a sudden pain.

"Zack, I think it's almost time. She wants to be born. Hold on little one. We don't have far to go. Give mama a bit of time, we will be in the right place soon."

"Come child, I can see your light is brighter than before. Langos, we need to go." Nana said and we rushed off.